WAR 7: PINK COTTON

FEB - - 2021
1

JE

WAR

SEVEN

Pink cotton

NATIONAL BESTSELLING AUTHOR

T. STYLES

By T. Styles

ARE YOU ON OUR EMAIL LIST?

SIGN UP ON OUR WEBSITE

www.thecartelpublications.com

OR TEXT THE WORD: CARTELBOOKS TO

22828

FOR PRIZES, CONTESTS, ETC.

Check Out Other Titles By The Cartel Publications

By T. Styles

WAR 7: PINK COTTON

WWW.THECARTELPUBLICATIONS.COM

By T. Styles

WAR 7
PINK COTTON
By
T. STYLES

Library of Congress Control Number: 2020905571

ISBN 10: 1948373122

ISBN 13: 978-1948373128

Cover Design: Book Slut Girl

First Edition
Printed in the United States of America

By T. Styles

What Up Fam,

This letter seems to be a lot heavier than I've been accustomed to writing in the past. As I type this we are currently under quarantine as a nation due to COVID-19 aka The Corona Virus. If anybody would have told me a couple months ago that we would have to stay home and the movie theatre's, bars, restaurants would be closed and the NBA, MLB and NCAA Tournaments would be canceled; I would have laughed them out. I can honestly say I could not imagine something like this happening in my lifetime. On the flip side, I know that EVERYTHING, good or bad, happens for a reason. Although folks are going crazy being in the house and trying to flatten the curve of this virus, the earth is healing.

It seems like we have done so much damage to the planet that we had to be put on punishment. Maybe when we are finally able to come out again, we won't take so much for granted. In the meantime, take this time to learn something new. Boost your immune system up with exercise, fruit and veggies and cherish your loved ones. It may come a time when all we have is each other ;)

I'm done preaching. So, without further delay, go on and escape into the world of the Wales' and Lou's! We gonna have soooooo much to talk about!!

With that being said, keeping in line with tradition, we want to give respect to a vet or new trailblazer paving the way. In this novel, we would like to recognize:

STORE CLERKS

FOOD/SUPPLY DELIVERY DRIVERS

TRUCK DRIVERS

HOSPITAL CUSTODIANS

DOCTORS & NURSES

ALL ESSENTIAL WORKERS

Anyone who works in these fields and more not named above, are on the front line of this virus. You brave souls are risking your health daily to keep us going! We truly appreciate what you do! God bless and protect you all.

By T. Styles

Aight Fam, I love ya'll and will talk to you again soon! God Bless!

Charisse "C. Wash" Washington

Vice President

The Cartel Publications

www.thecartelpublications.com

www.facebook.com/publishercwash

Instagram: publishercwash

www.twitter.com/cartelbooks

www.facebook.com/cartelpublications

Follow us on Instagram: Cartelpublications

#CartelPublications

#UrbanFiction

#PrayForCece

#ThankyouEssentialWorkers

#War7

By T. Styles

PROLOGUE
SPRING, 1972
VIRGINIA

Rain pounded on the Petit estate rattling the windows. Causing an eerie sound resembling horror music. Thirteen-year-old Angela continued to glance up at the chandelier believing it to be spectacular. Although beautiful, the gold and crystal fixture was just another one of the many delicate intricacies throughout the massive estate.

Yes, Gina spared no expense on her home, this much was true.

After all, every area in the mansion was cared for, loved and pampered by her only daughter. And yet as Angela ate dinner with her mother and father Morgan, she could see tiny webs entangled within the spokes, with small creatures crawling throughout. Despite the nonstop cleaning, dusting and buffing that Angela was forced to do daily, she smiled. Because failing to clean the piece thoroughly, and Gina not catching her error, meant she had gotten over on her domineering mother.

"Angie, did you hear me?"

Angela's gaze remained above.

"Angie!" Gina yelled, slamming her fork against the rose gold embroidered China plate. "Do you hear me talking to you?"

"Uh, yes, mother, I do."

Gina picked up her fork and stabbed at the cold steak on her plate. "I don't believe you. What did I say?"

What did she say? What did she say?

She tried to recall as she shoved around the green beans that were supposed to be cooked but were nowhere near done. Because on top of many things, Gina was a horrible cook.

"I heard you, mother." She said firmer. "I, I was just, I don't know, tired, I guess. But I'm listening."

"Good. Because people are talking. And I know you enjoy being in your own head but—"

"Oh, hun, leave the girl alone." Morgan grabbed an extra buttered role, the only edible food on the plate. He was a tall stout man with piercing blue eyes and a commanding voice. His tone was mostly fluff when it came to his family but when he gave orders on his airline, he was king. "Just leave her be. Besides, I'm tired of all the chatter."

"I won't leave her alone and you should be more serious, Morgan. You aren't the one who has to deal with her crazy spells."

14   *By T. Styles*

"I'm not crazy, mother." She said through a squinted gaze.

"Are you sure about that? Because the way you move around it's like, it's like you don't take life seriously."

"I don't wanna be grim all the time if that's what you mean." She smiled with all of her heart. "I want to live. I want to be happy."

"Well, crying and laughing while walking down the street alone is not being happy. You're portraying yourself like a mad woman. And embarrassing the hell out of this family in the process. I can't have that anymore. I will not have that anymore."

Angela appeared to black out again. Looking around, up and down. Everywhere but on her parents.

"Angie, are you listening?" Gina persisted.

Silence.

"Angie!"

"I was thinking of a song, mother."

"You don't think of a song while people are talking to you." She took a deep breath. "It's rude."

"But I do. I do it all the time."

She doesn't understand me. She doesn't get what I'm going through. If only she would stop being so—

"You're doing it again aren't you?"

She sipped her juice and took a deep breath. "Actually, I wanted to ask if I could, well, there's a party and I, I guess, I was wondering if you would let me go. If you do, I promise to be on my best behavior. And to do all I can to not embarrass the, the, the, the...Petit...Strand...uh..."

"Angela, calm down," Morgan said kindly. Whenever she was nervous she stuttered.

She nodded. "Yes, father."

Gina stared at her intensely.

Please say yes. Please say yes. Please—

"No." Gina said plainly.

"Why, mother?"

"Simply put, you aren't ready or stable."

Immediately Angela was overwhelmed with emotion. The toughest thing in the world was to get her mother to listen. Followed by saying the right thing. Because if she didn't 'sound' or 'act right', Angela's world could get extremely dark and lonely.

It happened many times before.

"Mother, I—." While talking she lifted her hand and accidently knocked over her juice. Making a

By T. Styles

horrible mess, immediately she jumped up and went about trying to clean up the table. Grabbing expensive linen napkins that soaked up the bright red color of the strawberry punch.

This is bad. This is bad.

"I'm so, so sorry, mother."

"You see," Gina said as her head raised high. "This is what I'm talking about." She sighed deeply. "You aren't fit to be in the dining room, let alone a party."

"It won't happen a—."

"Go to your room, Angie. I want to talk to your father. Alone."

"Mother, I—"

"Now!"

"Yes, mother."

Angela pushed back her chair softly and with her head held low, walked away. Each time her toes pressed into the recently polished wooden floor, she felt as if she were stepping deeper, further, into her own grave.

Angela woke up and walked toward the window in her room. From her view, straight ahead, she saw acres and acres of luscious green land surrounding the mansion. To the right was Mrs. Fischer's house and it was also spectacular. She was an older woman who refused to enter a nursing home despite her deteriorating health.

As a result, many came under the guise of helping her maintain her sprawling property, but they also helped themselves of her funds too. She didn't mind much; she didn't have children. Her motto had always been that she couldn't take the millions with her in death.

After slipping on her lavender colored robe, she walked to her bedroom door. She hadn't been given the okay to leave her room, but school was in an hour. So, peeking her head out she said very softly, "Mother."

Silence.

"Mother, are you up yet?"

Angela walked deeper into her house, down the long, dark hallway.

Normally she would hear whispering within the walls from either her sibling or her mother talking to her father. But today seemed eerily silent which

By T. Styles

was bad because during the quiet times she grew sad.

After searching the house everywhere, she made it to her parents' room. She knew it was best to go away and wait for her mother's call. And at the same time, she figured she must've driven her father to the airport, something she did from time to time when Morgan didn't feel like driving.

Before entering she hung at the doorway awhile. After all she had good reason. Her mother made it clear that it was unlawful to enter her private quarters without permission.

Looking to her right and left, she slowly pushed it open. Like most things in the house it creaked. Once the door was ajar, Angela took notice of the darkness she felt. It wasn't as clean as the rest of the house, because Angela wasn't allowed to enter and care for the space as she did everywhere else.

And so, Gina's room always held with it a strange odor. That of mothballs and cheap perfume. Which was confusing to say the least. She never understood why Gina was so cheap. The Petit family came from wealth and in Angela's mind wealth should be explored.

Instead, she and her brother were forced to wear secondhand clothing. Socks stitched at the *toe. Shoes tarred at the bottom and things of that nature. Outside of money spent on the home, it was as if Gina wanted to downplay her fortunes, at the expense of her children.*

Walking deeper into the massive room when she made it to her mother's side of the bed, she paused. There on a nightstand was a lamp on top of a white knit duster. Next to it was a red paperback. It was somewhat tattered and old, and it was obvious it had been read many times.

It was called BRAINWASH LOVE by Gemma Holmes.

Curious about its content she picked up the book and stuffed it in the back of her pants.

On foot, Angela was halfway to her school when she happened upon it a large group of yellow flowers in her neighbor's yard. With a smile on her face she brought one to her nose and inhaled its sweet fragrance. Suddenly she was at ease.

At peace.

By T. Styles

Shouldn't everyone experience its fragrance and beauty?

Wanting to share the moment, before she knew it, she plucked over twenty.

Once at school, she floated down the hallways and even into her class with a wide smile on her face. Almost as if she was a flower girl in a wedding. Passing them out one by one, her body tingled when those on the receiving end of her graciousness smiled.

She felt accomplished.

Giving was something she always wanted to do and yet she knew her acts of kindness would have to be reduced to the things that could be done for free. Because although she was rich, she was far from wealthy.

And there was a difference.

Later on, that day Angela sat in class with wide eyes. Whenever there was a question she would jump up and flail her arms left and right eager to answer.

But there was another side.

When she wasn't chosen, as always, she went wild and often cried. Her fellow classmates may have been used to her antics, but her teacher knew something was gravely wrong with Angela Petit.

"Angie, can I talk to you for a second?" Mrs. Forsett said.

Angela walked over to her, while waving at the kids leaving the classroom. "Yes, Mrs. Forsett."

"How, how are you today?" As she waited for an answer, her eyes roamed over Angela's frame.

"You didn't like the flowers?"

"Of, of course I liked them but…Angie, I—."

"Angela. I like Angela."

She nodded. "Okay, this isn't about the flowers. You seem excitable today. Did, did something happen at home?"

Angela smiled brightly but remained silent. Trying to stay calm as Gina warned.

"Angela, did something happen at home?" She asked firmer.

Suddenly huge tears rolled down her cheek. "Please, please don't tell my parents about today. I was only trying to be nice."

"Of, of course I won't tell them. I just want to make sure you're—"

"I'm fine. I'm…" Angela nodded awkwardly, hugged her and ran out the room.

Worried about messing up at school, Angela prepared a huge meal to gain favor with her family. There were pancakes, waffles, scrambled eggs along with bacon, sausage, and biscuits with gravy. She even insured that the table was set and ready.

But as she floated around there was one thing that she thought about constantly. Would she ruin the moment by angering her mother again?

And so, per usual, she always wanted things to go as planned.

She wanted to be the model daughter, like the beautiful blonde hair blue eyed girl on the box of Strands Inc. Ironically, that little girl was a younger version of herself. Gina didn't prefer her much now.

But she still tried.

Because she had no choice.

"What are you, what are you doing, Angela?" Gina asked walking into the kitchen.

Angela jumped. "Um...I..."

"What are you doing with all this?"

"I don't understand, I'm cooking dinner."

She frowned. "Angie, it's 10:00 o'clock at night."

She hadn't realized the time of day. Because like in the past she went with the mood swing, even if it took her too far. "Oh, uh, okay." She wiped her hands on her apron.

"So why are you making breakfast at 10:00 o'clock at night?"

Angela looked around. It was as if she was seeing her actions for the first time that day. A few moments ago, she was confident but now, she appeared disheveled and embarrassed.

Her eyes widened. "Well there's nothing wrong with breakfast in the evening, right?"

"That's not the point! This is what I'm talking about. Once again, your irrational moods impact everybody in this house. And your teacher told me what you did today. Picking at Mrs. Fischer's yard."

The teacher was a fucking snake.

At that moment her father came downstairs. He looked around for a second where he stood and then took a deep breath. "Honey, is everything okay?"

"Yes, father."

"Good." He clapped his hands once. "As long as you're fine."

Gina was livid at how much he appeared to protect Angela. "If you believe things are fine, you're

By T. Styles

sicker than she is. At this point I'm going to really need you to start taking things seriously. I'm trying to save our daughter's life. Because she can't do it herself."

"That may be true. But no matter what, she prepared a meal for the family. Now let's eat it together as one."

And so, everyone ate the breakfast food. To say Angela was a good cook was an understatement. Morgan preferred her food and still there was a weird air over the meal. And when she looked at her mother's eyes, she knew things would be changing.

She saw their shadows under her door.

She knew they would be coming, but still she hoped they would stay away. It would do her no good.

Suddenly the door flung open and she was yanked kicking and screaming off her bed by her father and brother. "No, please don't! I'll do better. I promise, I promise not to, not to act this way anymore!"

She was carried into the hallway.

"Daddy, please don't do this again! I'm begging you!"

She was taken up the stairs.

"Why are you listening to mother? Why are you doing this to me?"

"Just do your time," Hercules said as he continued to help carry her to the one place on earth Angela hated.

She could plead her heart out all she wanted.

Nothing could be done.

Besides, Gina made it perfectly clear that Morgan mustn't intervene with the rearing of the children. And so, she was taken higher within the mansion. Into the large attic called a garret. There was a mattress, pillow, blanket and large window.

She was thrown inside.

Landing on hand and knee, Angela jumped up and pounded on the door repeatedly. But it was closed and locked.

After exhausting herself for hours, she finally laid on the floor closest to the window overlooking the backyard. She could feel the book she stuffed in her underwear pressing firmly against her stomach.

By T. Styles

With tears pouring down her face she picked at the fluffy fiberglass installation on an exposed part of the floor, which resembled pink cotton.

CHAPTER ONE
JERSEY'S ESTATE
PRESENT DAY

Mason was pacing the floor rapidly. Unlike Preach who was still inside the room where Banks was having surgery, he couldn't wrap his mind around what was happening. Of course, he remembered the many times when Banks would have headaches, but things always seemed to work their way out.

Now after recalling the moments Mason felt foolish for not suggesting that he go to a doctor instead. But who was he kidding? Nobody told Banks what to do in life. He was his own man and the world knew it.

The stressful situation started yesterday, at the wedding reception, when Banks experienced a headache so severe, he was forced to sit down. It wasn't like Banks was new to the painful episodes. Since he was transitioning into a man, he was in agony a lot. So, most thought it had to do with his male hormone therapy. Even he did. But now, after learning from a doctor that he had a tumor, they were afraid of one thing and one thing only.

By T. Styles

That Banks Wales would die.

When the door to Banks' room opened an Preach walked out, Mason rushed up to him. "How is he?"

He wiped a hand down his face. "Man..., it's...it's..."

"Tell me something." Mason's energy was anxious and added fire to an already futile situation.

Preach sighed deeply. He experienced stress in his lifetime, but this was by far the worst ever. "It's hard to tell right now. I mean, they seem to know what they're doing but—."

"You have to tell me more than that!" Mason moved closer. "My friend is in there." He pointed at the door. "If something happens to him, I promise you, it won't be—"

"Don't look at things that way. We have to make sure we put only positive vibes in the air."

"You sound like your father." Mason walked away and turned back. "Do you, I mean, do you remember him complaining of headaches in the past?" He asked, running a hand down his face. "Because this shit is fucking me up. Like really."

"Headaches this bad? No. I mean he asked for a pill here and there but what we do is stressful already. To be honest, at the time, I'm thinking it's no more than that." He crossed his arms over his body tightly. "This...this..."

"I know, man."

"I feel like I should've tried to put the press on him."

"Preach, you have a family. You couldn't be around him twenty-four seven. None of us could."

"I know but—."

"Seriously. Can you imagine trying to get him to go to the doctors? Even when he was hit with the last headache, he didn't want the help. It was the final thing he said."

"True but—."

"All I know is he's gonna survive, because I will never be able to bury him. Ever. It's not in me, Preach."

When he heard a sudden rush of loud voices Mason walked into the large foyer. There at the door was a very much pregnant Jersey. She was angry and Mason's soldiers were doing their best to contain her.

But it wasn't working.

"What's happening, Jersey?" Preach asked. "Are you in trouble?"

By T. Styles

"Can you tell me what the fuck is going on, Mason?" Her chest rose and fell heavily.

"I'll talk to her." Mason said to Preach and the group.

When everyone left the scene, she moved closer. "Mason, what's going on with Banks? Why was he taken from the house and why won't people talk to me? I've been worried sick. "

"It's too early to tell right now."

"Nigga, what does that even mean?"

"Right now, I want you to go home." He put his hands-on her shoulders to push her out the door. "I'll call—."

"So, you gonna kill Banks' baby?" She rubbed her large belly. "By handling me roughly? Is that what you're actually about to do?"

He wanted to steal her in the face and drop her instead. "Come with me and I'll tell you everything you want to know."

They were sitting on the sofa in the living room of the house Banks built for Jersey. And it was time to break the news, but he decided to do it slowly. "First off, how you feeling?" He examined her quickly and she looked like an emotional wreck.

Jersey rubbed her belly and sighed. She was due any day and the stress with Banks was too much to endure. "I'm not doing good, Mason."

"I know." He paused and ran his hand down his thighs. "I know, all of this shit, whatever it is, is fucked up."

"If you know this, why won't you let anyone talk to me?"

"I'm trying. This is hard."

"The last thing I knew we were having a wedding reception and the next thing I know Banks is being taken away. I can't eat or sleep, Mason. I just want the truth." She removed her phone from her purse and pointed the screen his way. "I've called him at least fifty times and no answer." Huge tears fell down her cheeks. "And it's, it's fucking killing me! I have to know." She dropped her phone in her purse.

Seeing his wife distraught over another man stung a bit. It was clear, if never before, that she was into him hard. And at the same time, they both held this weird connection. Because at the end of the day they cared about Banks Wales.

And they wanted him alive.

Mason moved uneasily and took a deep breath. It was as if it were the hardest thing he ever had to say in his life. "He's having surgery."

She shook her head slowly, and a smile spread across her face, believing the man to be joking. "Surgery? That...that doesn't make any sense."

"I know."

Her eyebrows rose. "Mason, you're fucking scaring me."

"I'm sorry about that."

"Don't be sorry! If he were having surgery, he would let me know." She placed a hand over her heart. "And he wouldn't do that when we are just days away from, from having our baby."

"You knew about the headaches, right? You knew about all the times he complained of pain?"

She shook her head no although she meant yes. "You mean the tension headaches?"

He shrugged. "If that's what you call them. All I know is apparently shit was worse than he knew. And I hate to put it on you, but if you ask me, you should've forced him to get help sooner."

She sat back slowly. "Mason, that's not fair."

"Might not be fair but it's the truth. You sleep with the man every night! Every fucking night. Not me! So yeah, this is on you."

She hated his attitude and at the same time he alone held information she needed. Which meant he alone held the power. "Even with the headaches, I never, I never knew something more was going on. Definitely nothing warranting surgery."

"I'm going to be honest...we have some people taking care of him now."

She stood up and took a deep breath. "Okay, where is he at?"

"Um..."

"Mason, which hospital? Because I have to be with him."

"I think you should go home."

"You know that ain't happening. The only question is are you taking me to where he is or do I have to take myself?"

He remained seated and looked up at her. "He's not at a hospital. I mean...he's not at..."

She frowned. "Mason, I'm having a really bad day. The last thing I need is a run around. Now, where is he?"

"Listen, the stress on the baby can't be good. When I find out something—"

"If you think I'm leaving you don't know me at all. I'm staying. And the only thing I need to know right now is where is my husband?"

He glared. As far as he knew, they were playing house and that was the extent of their situation. "Ya'll got married?"

"No, I mean not yet." She looked down. "But it is happening. You need to get used to that fact."

He shrugged. "What the fuck you talking about? About to get married and being married are two different things." The relief he felt that they weren't wed was huge.

"I mean we're living our lives as a couple, Mason."

He laughed.

"Fuck so funny?" She asked.

"Living your life as a couple ain't the same!"

"I know that."

"Good."

"Is it me or are you acting jealous? Cause it ain't like you don't have a girlfriend. What's her name again? Dasher?"

He smirked. "I'm not going there with you. At the end of the day, if we keeping it one hundred,

I've known the man for most of my life. That's all I'm saying."

"And I haven't known him long?"

Mason laughed because the conversation was going nowhere. "I'm not even going to dignify that shit with a response. You and me both know what it is."

"You know what, this shit is stupid."

"Agreed." He said.

"So where is Banks?"

He looked toward the back of the house and then at Jersey. "He's, uh, he's in the room."

"The room? But I thought he needed surgery."

"He does."

"So, when he going to his appointment?"

"Now."

She frowned. "Is he late?"

"No. It's happening now."

"Wait, are you actually telling me he's having surgery in my house?"

He shrugged.

"What is wrong with you?" She threw her hands up in the air. "What if he dies? What if, what if something goes wrong? I'm not going to bury him because you being stupid!"

He quickly stood up and slapped her. It was a reflex, but the damage was done.

"I can't believe you did that shit." She said holding the side of her face. "You, you actually put your hands on me."

"It's not the first time."

"Wow...I'm so fucking glad I left you."

"Get outta here." He waved her away.

"If Banks is here, I'm—."

"Jersey, you gonna make me hurt you."

"I caution you against that."

"Are you threatening me?" He asked.

"YES, NIGGA! I'M FUCKING THREATENING YOU!"

Silence.

She stepped closer. "Do you think I won't react back?" She said in a low tone. "Don't you remember? It was me who killed two police officers. What you think I'll do if you keep me from the one man who has been there for me in ways you never have?"

He laughed to prevent from snapping. "You talking reckless now."

"Am I?"

Silence.

"What I know is this...you won't keep me from him, Mason." She continued. "It will never work."

"I'm not going to tell you again to get out." He said pointing over her shoulder.

She took a deep breath. "I'm leaving for now." There was no sense in trying to reach him and she knew it. "But I'll be back later."

"You can but you won't get inside."

"We'll see about that. Because in case you forgot, this is my fucking house! And contrary to what you might think, I'm king!"

Rev was in bed, trying to get over a bad cold. His girlfriend, Banana, nicknamed so because of her light skin and curvy body, walked inside their bedroom and placed a red cup of hot tea on the table by the lamp.

Grabbing the digital thermometer, she checked his temperature. "It's 101.3. Your fever seems to be going up."

"I'll be fine," he sighed. "It just has to work its way through me I guess."

By T. Styles

She nodded and smiled although her expression showed great concern. "I hear you."

He sat up and she adjusted the pillows behind his back to provide him comfort. Handing him the tea he took a sip. "It's just a cold, Banana. Try not to worry."

She nodded. "Why do I get the impression something else is on your mind?"

"It is. Banks is having surgery today."

Her eyebrows rose. "Oh, honey, I'm sorry. I know how much you care about him and his father. How is he?"

He coughed and covered his mouth with his elbow. "I'm waiting on Preach to tell me now."

"She touched his leg. Preach has to be going crazy. He loves him as much as you do."

"Exactly. And with my youngest son dying of cancer if something happens to Banks, he'll..." His cell phone rang. "Hand me that." She did and he looked at the screen. "It's Preach."

"I'll let you take it." She kissed him on the head and walked out.

He coughed. "How's Banks?"

"I don't know, dad." His voice sounded anxious. "And I'm...worried."

He was too. "Banks is strong. He'll pull out of this."

"You have to see his face. He doesn't look the same. It's like—."

"Listen, when you and Banks grew close, I welcomed it because I know he's a good man and around your age. But one of the things I told you is that in life, what needs to happen will always occur. Even if we don't understand why. And it is our response to things and how we handle the situation, that will judge our moods and our lives."

Preach took a deep breath. "You're right."

"Banks will be fine, Preach. I didn't promise his father I would take care of him just for him to die." He coughed. "Now give me the address."

"Are you sure you should be leaving the house? You sound like you're getting worse and it could be dangerous."

"Give me the address. I'm on my way."

CHAPTER TWO
THE PETIT ESTATE

The day called for slightly warm weather...

But Gina Petit, whose blood ran ice cold, walked through the door of her estate holding her grandsons Walid and Ace in car seats. What a difference years made. The mansion was falling apart and was a long way from how it was in the beginning. Time and lack of attention showed through the cracked paint and warped paneling on the floor.

The estate looked, well, creepy.

The moment she crossed the threshold her eldest son Hercules rushed up to her. His energy was anxious and threatening but she was used to this behavior when it came to him.

"Mother, where on earth have you been?"

"Out."

"Out?! Everyone has been losing it around here." He ran his hand through his short cropped blond hair so quickly it was as if he wanted to snatch it off. He was in his early sixties but still held onto his boyishly good looks.

"Hercules, don't talk to me like you're my father. You and me both know it won't bode well for my mood."

"I'm grown. I can talk how I feel."

She thought he was cute sometimes. "I appreciate your overprotectiveness. But I've told you before I won't stand for it in the past and I won't stand for it now."

He had better calm down if he wanted to get through her tough exterior. "Mother, you've been gone for months. Didn't even think to reach out. Do you realize what we've been going through? Trying to get the police involved even though they seemed skeptical?"

"That's because they knew where I was." She shrugged.

"Why?"

"Because I saw no reason to exhaust policeman hours in the event you called, so I let them know the situation."

"You tell the police and not me?" He threw his hands up. "What sense does that make when you rely on me for everything, mother?"

"They can handle things better, Hercules."

"Mother, you sound like a fool."

"I had to do what I had to do. Understand that if secrecy wasn't important, I would not have been gone for so long and you would have been aware. But when you're dealing with people with money at their disposal, anonymity is of the highest order."

Hercules looked at the babies with great suspicion. "Who are they? You can at least tell me that."

"Your nephew's." She walked over to the tattered brown sofa and placed them on the couch gently inside of their designer car seats.

"Nephews?" He frowned. "That makes no sense."

"Well, your grand nephews."

"Again, that makes no sense."

"Not everything needs to be broken down. Let's just say they are of your bloodline and we'll leave it at that for now."

"Of course, mother." He rolled his eyes.

"Don't be sarcastic."

When the maid came to retrieve the babies, Gina plucked off her shoes. Staying with Banks under the guise of being a nanny was stressful over the passing months. As a result, it did terrible things to her mental health.

And it was her own fault.

After all, Gina was an older woman, in her seventies, who didn't have the stamina to keep up a lie for so long and yet that's exactly what she did.

"What I want you to understand is this, what I'm doing, I'm doing for our family, Hercules." She removed her wig exposing another wig looking type mess.

"Oh, so you want to talk now?"

"Hercules!"

"Mother, this charade has gone on for too long. you do realize, that don't you? Going around the bush when you're obviously going to have me clean up your mess is a waste of time."

"For the sake of time, I'll tell you I found my granddaughter."

"First off, I found Banks not you." He glared as he stood over her. "Secondly, don't you mean your grandson?"

She glared. "You know what I mean."

"Actually, mother, I don't."

"Hercules, he was born female. That's all I'm saying."

"So, wait, back to what you said, he had children of his own?" Hercules asked. "Like...did he give birth to them?"

44

"No. But I'll get into that later. For now, where is Carmen?" She looked around from where she sat.

"That's what I've been trying to tell you. Carmen has been missing for almost as long as you have. Nobody knows where she is. At first, I thought she was with you but since it's obvious she's not I'm confused. And at this point, highly concerned."

Gina rose. "This doesn't make any sense. Why would she leave without telling us?"

"I'm not sure. She was in the house and the next thing I know she left. But if you ask me it's like mother like daughter."

She glared. "Don't be sarcastic, Hercules. This is serious."

"Exactly. Which is why I want answers about what you've been doing outside of kidnapping."

"Not now. I'm exhausted. I'm going to make a few phone calls to try and find out where she is. In the meantime, we'll figure all of this out."

Marshall walked into the master's suite where Gina had just gotten out of the shower. He was a young thing about twenty-seven with brunette hair. The saddest part of it all, was that he was nothing more than a glorified sex toy and he hated it.

Wearing grey sweatpants, no shirt, he crossed his arms over his chest. "I'm not even going to ask you where you've been."

She wrapped her towel tighter around her waist and flopped on the edge of the bed. "Are you sure about that?"

"Well, since you're being cynical, you can't go about the world thinking you don't owe anybody an answer. We have been worried sick."

"Wait, is this the part where you *aren't* asking me where I've been? Because if it is, I can't tell."

He dropped his arms and walked deeper into the room. "Okay, so I lied. But if you—"

"Marshall, the last thing I need right now is nagging. So, if you want to argue you won't get any of my attention or time. But if you want to help me find my daughter, who I asked you to look over in the first place, then we can talk."

Marshall crossed his arms over his chest. He knew fully well what his job requirements were. To fuck Gina like she like to be fucked. And to remain voiceless regarding the family.

He had been doing it since he was eighteen and yet he was tiring of such a mundane role in life. But what could he do? He didn't have access to her wealth. In fact, she had him on an allowance so small, he could barely afford to take himself out to eat. For a grown man, it was almost as if he wasn't getting paid at all.

"I don't know where she is."

She smirked. "Wow, I would think since you're fucking her too, that you would know more."

He was shocked.

How had she known?

"I didn't...I never...touched your daughter!"

"Come now," she laughed lightly. "She's a younger, prettier version of me. How could you not want to fuck? But she's also a broker version of me too."

"Can I do anything for you?"

She crawled in bed and removed the towel that was wrapped around her body. Dropping it on the floor she said, "First thing I want you to do is come over here and get down to business."

"Gina..."

She opened her legs wide. "Marshall, that means keeping your lips together until you're down low."

"Can we talk first?"

She opened her legs further apart, showcasing the hairy grey mound that had grown out of control. And as if he couldn't see it already, she spread her pussy lips so the pink center could shine through. "We will talk after you relax me. Because trust me, I'm not in a good mood. And we both know what happens, when I'm not in a good mood now don't we?"

He did.

His allowance would be cut down even more.

So, without hesitation, he walked toward the bed. Crawling on top of her soft flesh, he pressed his body against hers. He weighed heavily due to anger, but she could take the pressure.

Snaking his hands behind her cheeks, he spread them apart lightly and pounded his dick inside of her with brutal force. Almost as if he knew the code to make her cum quicker. Some would say he did, after all, he had been fulfilling her needs for years.

Enjoying herself greatly, she moaned and said his name repeatedly as she ran her red fingernails across the flesh of his back.

"Marshall, I've almost arrived! I've almost arrived!"

Wanting off of her, he pumped a few more times until she finally reached ecstasy. Pulling his dick out, he wiped it with his hand.

"That was great."

Out of her view, he rolled his eyes.

"Now, tell the kids it's time for a family meeting." She eased up, sat on the edge of the bed and grabbed her towel off the dusty floor. "We have a lot to discuss before the end of the day."

The table was dressed in a cloth so old and tattered it needed to be thrown away. As always, since her husband passed, Gina sat at the helm of the table. She was so stingy that per usual, they ate whatever was cheapest. That meant anything in boxes or cans. In fact, she considered fresh to be frozen and even that was done only on special occasions.

With Aaron, her other son, Hercules and Marshall waiting for the word as they stood around the table, she took a deep breath. "Everyone take a seat. I'll try to make this as quick as possible so we can eat."

Slowly they obeyed.

Wiping her pinched lips with an old cream cloth she said, "After Angela died, I felt as if my world would be rocked. And in some ways, it was. But now I have a chance to do right by her, by doing right by her children."

"Wait, she has more than one child?" Hercules asked. "Because as far as I know it was just Banks Wales."

"Blakeslee is her birth name."

"Mother."

"Don't mother me! You so busy being condescending that you miss my message. Of course, she didn't have more than one child. I'm referring to the twins and Minnesota. After all, they are, her grand*children*.

"Mother, that part is true." Hercules said throwing his hands up. "But I'm concerned at how you've gone about getting them. I'm also concerned about your purpose. And your plan."

Aaron knew where his brother was going and was feeling uncomfortable. At the end of the day he was concerned about the millions that were sitting in accounts accruing big interest and having to share with others if Gina ever died.

"Hercules, if mother feels the need to do this then maybe we should stay out of her way."

"You were always one for sucking up."

"Says the man who gets mad every time things don't go his way."

"I won't play mother's games again." He sipped his red wine.

"Stay out of the past." Aaron said. "Let's focus on now."

"Stand up for once in your life. Before mother's plans take a turn for the worse."

"I haven't shared any plans with you, Hercules." Gina said. "And I know what you're insinuating. But had it not been for me Angela would have been dead a long time ago. And had she not escaped; she would be still alive. So, whether you want to believe it or not, sometimes mother does know best."

"That still doesn't give you the right to—"

"My goal is simple. To be there for Banks, Minnesota and Spacey. And bring them here if they need to lie low. Since, based on the way they cleaned out the wedding reception, I have a feeling something is up."

"Why Spacey? He has no direct bloodline to us."

"He's loved by Banks. And that makes him loved by me."

THE PETIT ESTATE
1972

The nights were long and heavy. Angela, still alone in the garret, finally had an idea for an escape. Using the pin in her hair, she decided to pop the lock. Sliding out of bed, her bare feet pressed into the wooden paneling as she moved toward the door.

She was just about to get to work when Gina walked inside. She was wearing a red and white polka dot circle dress. Her blond hair pushed up in a neat bun.

Angela quickly placed the pin behind her back. "Hello, mother."

She glared. "What are you doing?"

"N...nothing."

Gina frowned and walked behind her. Forcing her hand open she removed the hair pin. "What is this for, Angie?"

"My hair."

"So why is it in your hand?"

Silence.

"You're trying to destroy me aren't you, Angie? You think because you're the face of Strands Inc Serum that I'll let you bring down what I've built."

"I never wanted to be the face of the business, mother!" She said placing a hand over her heart. "You used me when I was younger, by lying to people. I had brain tumors removed but you told everyone it was cancer! And then you cut my hair, claiming it grew back due to that stupid serum when—."

Gina slapped her face. "You are trying to destroy me." She pointed in her direction. "I was right."

A rush of heat ripped through Angela's pores. "I don't want to be here anymore."

"You will be here until you realize what it means to be a Petit."

"And what does being a Petit mean?" She asked trembling. "Is it to be ruled by you forever?"

"My bloodline came from my pussy and so it will always belong to me. You'll see."

It was midnight when a meal was pushed into the garret where Angela lie on the floor. The upper part of the house held a lot of heat, and as a result, laying on the floor was cooler. Gina had recently covered some of the exposed pink fiberglass. At first Angela thought it was to make the place nicer, since she was forced to live there. But after a while it was obvious her purpose was different. She was concerned that if she yelled and they had guests, they would hear her voice.

Still, a meal was welcomed.

Besides, she hadn't eaten in days. And so, the moment the door closed, and the meal was inside, she quickly tore into the food. It was a mixture of rice and ground beef and it smelled delicious.

By T. Styles

Instead of being satisfied, immediately she felt dizzy and off balance. Standing in the middle of the floor, her body swayed from left to right. It was obvious she was poisoned.

"I am your mother. But I'm also a powerful woman. You will come to understand this, or you will die."

Angela tried to sit down, instead she fell face first onto the floor.

CHAPTER THREE
MYRIO'S RESIDENCE

Minnesota sat on the balcony of Myrio's house overlooking his yard. Unfortunately, due to her nerves she picked up a nasty habit of smoking cigarettes but there was no way to stop. They soothed her because after witnessing her father murder Tobias, she was confused. As far as she could tell he was loyal, but more importantly he was the plug's son.

Didn't this mean suicide for the Wales and Louisville families?

She was on her fifth cigarette when Myrio walked out texting on his phone. His fingers slid over his screen effortlessly as he typed a message. Looking up at her once he said, "I know you not still fucked up 'bout that shit."

"Myrio, please..."

"Please what?" He stopped texting.

She took a pull and breathed out smoke. "Why is it that you don't act like you care about anything?"

"Not true." He continued to text again. "I care sometime." He breathed out. "I mean, uh, are you okay?"

"Not really." She shrugged. "But what can I do? My father did what he did, I guess. Although I wish I knew why."

He dropped his cell phone into his pocket. "Do you really wanna hear what I think?"

"Yes." She wanted to be left alone but he never let her be. It was as if he was guarding a precious jewel, that he was concerned would be stolen.

He sighed deeply. "When we first moved from our father's house to the projects, I thought it would be over for my family. I mean, we had everything and in one day it was gone."

She frowned. They talked a lot, but he never expressed his living conditions. "I didn't know you lived in the projects." Minnesota could not fathom the experience because since she was born, she had been a millionaire.

"That's because the past is not something I advertise. But when my father married a new woman he moved out and decided not to take his kids or his wife, I thought it would be over for us. Instead my mother stepped up."

She took another pull. "What did she do?"

He moved closer. "Whatever she had to do to be honest."

Minnesota looked at him a little harder. "I mean did she get a job or..."

"You know what she did to make cash."

He was annoying. With Tobias' death it was like the lights were turned on and he was suddenly not so attractive.

"Was she a prostitute?"

"I wouldn't call it a prostitute. She got one of those websites and had her own clients. We never saw anyone that she dealt with. She was good about trying to separate us from that part of her life. But we knew the deal. 'Cause we went from living in a fucked-up condition to living someplace better than where we lived with my father. The money was so good, that he tried to come back." He shook his head and laughed as if he could remember the time clearly. "Left the woman he was with and everything. Only for my mother to get him strung out on heroin. For revenge."

"Okay, I understand you gotta do what you gotta do but selling your body is a bit much to me."

"Don't judge what you don't know. If you're in that position, you don't know what you would be willing to do. Humans will adapt to whatever scenario they're given to survive."

"I'm sorry. I didn't mean to disrespect your mother."

"No apology necessary. Anyway, like I said, she did what she had to. At first, she didn't think she was strong enough. She thought she would fall when my father left but she not only rose up, she put us in a better position than when we started. And I see that with you."

"I don't know about all that." She looked down.

"I do. Banks takes you as a joke. But you will be the one who saves this family. You'll be the one who eventually saves him, if he's still around."

She rolled her eyes. At first, he seemed to idolize Banks but now that they were beefing, he took pride in going off about every detail.

"Can you please stop talking about my father?"

"All I know is this, after he killed Tobias, he wasn't concerned about you. And the heat shit would bring with Bolero. So why should you be concerned about him?"

"By me do you really mean us?"

"I hate when you do that. Just 'cause I want to see you win doesn't mean it's the only reason for me wanting to help." He grabbed her hand. "I just feel like you have to know who you really are that's all. And until you do, it's my duty to show you."

She looked down. "I'm scared. I helped my father out here and there but...but I've never really done anything like sell drugs. I mean, what if I make things worse if I approach Bolero?"

"Again, you're acting like I'm not going to be with you. You won't be alone. No step of the way."

"You may be with me but it's still my responsibility. I'll be the face of this shit. If I step to Bolero and I'm not correct he'll kill me and me alone."

"That's not what you're really worried about is it, Minnesota?"

She looked up at him. "That's not the only thing I'm concerned about."

"Tell the truth. The only thing you're worried about is Banks." He walked away and leaned against the house. "What I want to know is why? When it's so clear he doesn't care about you."

"Don't say that!"

"I'm serious! Banks is doing exactly what my father did to me." He placed his hand over his heart. "He has a whole new family. His friends don't even fuck with you. I guarantee that if you called, Mason wouldn't come to your rescue.

By T. Styles

Because he doesn't give a fuck. Banks is even having a fucking little girl because you weren't good enough." He rushed up to her and grabbed her hands. "Don't you see, baby? He's trying to replace you. He's trying to replace your brothers too."

His words rang true.

Minnesota took a deep breath. She was torn to say the least. On one end she believed what Myrio was saying was correct. And on the other end her father was her world. Even with killing Bolero's son, she knew he could take care of himself. She knew he could protect her too. Besides, she'd seen it many times before.

But what if Banks finally crossed the line by killing Tobias?

What if this was the end of the road? Wasn't it best to jump ship and save herself, instead of drowning in Banks' misery alone?

"Listen, let's not think about this right now." He kissed her cheek. "You look like you're famished. Let's grab something to eat."

She was relieved to get to anyplace else. At the moment she was so emotionally drained that she didn't even bother to put on a fresh beat.

"Famished huh?" She said playfully.

He winked and slapped her butt cheek. "Go to your car. I'll meet you there in a minute." He removed his phone and made a call.

She nodded and walked into the house, through the corridor and toward the silver Aston Martin he purchased for her in his driveway. Once inside the vehicle, she clutched the steering wheel tightly. Suddenly the severity of what she was dealing with hit her all at once. She was actually about to betray her father.

Myrio slid into the front passenger's seat and looked at her tank. "Why you ain't got gas?"

"I don't know."

He shook his head. "Let's go. We'll stop at the station."

"I...I can't right now."

He threw himself back and dragged a hand down his face. "What's wrong now? Because I can't keep promising you the world if you don't trust me."

"I...I mean...I just need five seconds." She looked toward the backseat.

"Five seconds for what?"

"My nerves are shook. I mean, can you hand me my purse? I need another cigarette."

"How much longer you gonna have this habit? Because I'm sick of smelling smoke on your skin and shit."

"I don't know...I mean for now it calms me down. I'm gonna quit soon."

He smirked.

"I'm serious, Myrio. Just, just a few more days."

With much attitude, he reached in the back and snatched her Louis Vuitton purse. Throwing it in her lap he said, "take a few puffs and smash that shit out. I have a long day planned and this weak shit you about ain't for me."

"I know."

"You keep saying you know when I been told you that we good. So, if you knew you wouldn't be upset. But it's cool, I'm gonna get you together whether you want me to or not. I'm..."

As he continued to talk, his words faded away.

He was still speaking, but for some reason she could no longer hear his voice. Besides, he seemed preachy, pushy and it caused her body to tremble. And suddenly, without even thinking, she reached into her purse, grabbed her .22 and shot him in the belly.

BOOM.

There was SILENCE.

A deafening SILENCE that felt surreal.

It wasn't until blood poured from his flesh that her eyes widened. With her fingertips covering her lips, she whispered, "Oh my, oh my God."

Let's be clear.

This was not a planned murder. She had all intentions of calming her nerves with a cigarette. But for some reason she felt she would be calmer if he was not around. If she didn't hear his voice. If she didn't hear his constant bickering and bossing her around.

And so, she took a life.

DOCTOR'S OFFICE

Jersey was seated waiting for her appointment. Unfortunately, Banks would usually be with her but now she was in a bad way.

She was alone.

The fact that her fiancé was having a mysterious surgery that Mason didn't want to tell her about, pushed her toward a breakdown.

By T. Styles

Everything was insane. The scenario of Banks not being in the picture never occurred. She wasn't the single mother type. And yet she was facing the possibility of being just that.

Jersey was so distraught that she started to dismiss her doctor's appointment all together. And then she felt her little girl kick within her womb. She may have been in love with Banks, but she was also giving life. And since It was her first daughter, she took that seriously.

"Are you okay?" A woman asked sitting next to her. She looked to be nine months pregnant and her blue eyes stared at her with sincerity. "You, you look like you're having a bad time. I'm sorry if I'm being too forward."

Jersey sniffled. She hadn't realized her anxious mood was apparent by those around. "I'm not doing well."

The woman scanned the office from where she sat. "Do you have anyone who can sit with you? I mean, are you waiting on someone else to arrive?"

Jersey thought about her life.

Her ex-husband was posted up in the house purchased for her by Banks, his best friend. One of her two surviving sons, Derrick, refused to talk to her. She hadn't seen Howard in forever and

Banks was getting surgery in what she deemed to be a backyard operation.

"No, I don't. I mean, I do but he, he can't be here right now because..." She suddenly busted out in laughter to prevent from crying. "It's all too ridiculous to be real."

"Well, is there anything I can do for you? I mean I know I don't know you. But I know how it feels to be alone. Sometimes when you're alone it's good to unload on a stranger."

"I wouldn't want to do that to you."

"It's okay. Really."

Jersey rubbed her belly. What did she have to lose? "My fiancé is having surgery and I'm not allowed to be there to support. And the person who is...who is in charge of the surgery is, well, I don't know, jealous of me."

"Sounds overwhelming."

"It is."

She nodded and took a deep breath. "Sometimes getting advice from outside sources is all that's needed."

She sniffled. "Like I said, it ain't happening."

"I'm a single mother." She looked down at her swollen belly. "And when I first told my family they took it hard."

By T. Styles

Someone coughed across the way.

"Why?"

"Because I'm pregnant in my forties." The woman continued. "It's frowned upon as you can imagine."

"Wow, I never thought about people's opinions because I'm older too."

"It was bad for me. If you don't have to go through that you're lucky because at least you have some support. Anyway, when I finally told my closest friends I was relieved at the amount of love I received."

Jersey shook her head. "It won't be the same because my situation is so much deeper. A lot of hate. A lot of, just a lot of emotions." She thought about having a baby with her ex-husband's best friend and felt like a whore.

"Still, there has to be someone in your life who can step up and help you sort things out. After all, you're about to be a new mom. Whatever this is that is trying to drag you down, you don't want to go at it alone."

"I mean, I, I do have sons."

The woman sat back, slightly relieved that maybe her life wasn't as bleak. "Good, what about reaching out to one of them? Are they adults? Do they live in the area?"

Jersey nodded yes.

"I suggest after this appointment you go see them. I don't care what kind of problems you're dealing with; no man can resist helping his mother."

THE LOUISVILLE ESTATE

Two hours later Jersey, still frantic, was at the Louisville estate uninvited. The moment she crossed over the threshold she heard Shay and Derrick fighting in the hallways. Sending echo filled negative energy throughout the property. Their beefs were a common issue but since they didn't have a relationship there was no way to help her son work things out.

Feet slapping down the hallway on the way to the bar, he was shocked when he saw his mother in the foyer.

By T. Styles

"What you doing here, ma?" He looked down at her huge belly and experienced more irritation.

"I need to talk to you."

"About what though?" He approached.

"Is the pregnancy okay?" Shay asked, walking up behind him. "Is dad in the car?" She continued. "Because I called him earlier and couldn't get an answer."

Jersey took a deep breath and repositioned herself a little. "I'm not sure where he is, Shay."

She frowned. "What does that mean?"

She directed her attention to her son. "Derrick, something is going on with Banks. Something, something bad."

Shay frowned. "What, what you mean something is going on with my father? I talked to him at the wedding and—."

"I don't have a lot of details. I'm sorry. But I do know that I'm not allowed to see him and he may be having surgery."

Shay placed her hand over her heart that thumped wildly in her chest. "Okay, which hospital is he in?"

Jersey tried to hold back her tears, but it was difficult. The only good part of the day was that her little girl was growing healthily in her womb.

"They're not at a hospital. I mean, that's what Mason told me anyway."

Shay moved closer. "Are you playing games?"

"Do I look like I'm in any position to play?"

"So, if he's not at a hospital where is he?"

"That's why I'm here. I need help. Because whatever surgery Banks is having its being done at, well, my house."

THE WALES ESTATE

Spacey was at the Wales Estate grabbing some of his belongings. Since he was now a married man, he knew he would spend less time at his childhood home and more time with his wife. He knew he would have to put aside being a kid in exchange for being a man in the future, but for now he enjoyed having two homes.

He was almost fully packed when Joey walked in and leaned against the doorway. "So, you actually moving out on your own huh?"

By T. Styles

"Yep, but this is me getting prepared for our honeymoon now." He paused. "The real question is are you moving back?"

Joey sighed deeply. "Yeah, I gotta stay away from the people I rolled with before if I'm gonna have my recovery stay a success."

"I'm proud of you, man."

Joey tried to hide the pride he felt upon hearing those words from his older brother. "You told me that already. Stop being mushy."

Spacey laughed. "Well there's nothing wrong with telling you again is it? I could always just ignore your ass and see how that feels."

Joey laughed. "Well I wish you could be—"

Spacey's phone rang, interrupting his brother's sentence.

Joey chuckled. "You better hurry up and get home. Looks like your wife is hitting you up again."

Spacey frowned and glared at the screen. "Nah, this Shay's number."

Joey stood up straight. "Shay? I just spoke to her about an hour ago when she hit me about her and Derrick fighting. What she want now?"

"I don't know." Spacey answered the call. The moment he did Shay was crying loudly. "Hold up, I can barely hear you."

"I'm...I'm sorry but—."

"Shay, calm down and tell me what's going on."

She took several deep breaths although it didn't help. "It's dad, he's having surgery!"

Spacey's body erected as he experienced a painful reaction. Up until that moment he never considered losing *both* parents. "What you talking about having surgery? Pops ain't tell me none of that shit."

Joey walked fully into the bedroom. "What's wrong, man?" He whispered.

Spacey ignored him as he continued to focus on the call. "Shay, tell me exactly what's happening."

"All I know is that he's having some procedure at Jerseys estate. You gotta get over there right away. I'm scared!"

Rev walked into Jersey's Estate when Preach let him inside. The moment the door closed, Preach hugged his father tightly. When his eyes rested on him fully, his heart dropped. "Dad, you look bad."

By T. Styles

He nodded. "Where's the living room?" He coughed. "I have to sit down."

"No, let me take you to one of the bedrooms instead."

Rev wasn't feeling well so he obeyed. Five minutes later he was in one of Jersey's guestrooms under the covers. He coughed again. "How are you, son?"

"It's...you know...not good."

He nodded. "Any word on Banks' condition yet?"

"No. The doctors are with him but we're still waiting. But I'm glad you're here."

Rev coughed insanely and Preach breathed deeply.

"Me too, son. Me too."

CHAPTER FOUR

Mason cruised in his BMW sipping whiskey. He was in the middle of one of the longest days of his life. He was literally waiting to hear if his best friend would survive an operation. The fact that death was even a possibility took him to terrible levels emotionally. And at the same time this was his current life.

At the end of the day he would have to be strong or fall next to him.

When his phone rang, he looked over at the passenger seat and saw it was Dasher. In the past he felt like the luckiest man alive to have a woman like her on his arm. After all she resembled his first love, Blakeslee, which eerily made him want her more. He even found himself thinking of the future and starting all over.

And then everything changed when Tobias was killed.

When he saw the blood pour from his wound, he realized his death took every hope he had for the future. And as a result, he wasn't sure if he was feeling her anymore.

By T. Styles

Still, he hit the button so that the call would connect to his speaker phone. "What's up?" He continued to maneuver the car. "Because you hit me at the worst possible time."

"Says you every time I reach out."

He wasn't feeling like playing. "Dasher, I'm serious."

"And so am I. I mean, I've been trying to reach you, Mason. Why haven't you returned any of my calls? It seems selfish if you ask me."

He sat deeper in his soft grey leather seat. "I don't mean to be selfish. It's just that I'm dealing with a lot."

"Okay, let me hear it."

He shook his head. "Nah."

"Mason, if you're dealing with something you should feel as though you can tell me. We are together remember?"

"Listen, you young."

"Oh, now my age a problem? 'Cause you don't seem to have an issue when we fuck. Or I'm sucking your dick."

He passed a slow refrigerated water truck. "Why you talking crazy? Huh? You know how I feel about the language."

"I'm serious."

"And so am I! And I know you there. You tell me enough. But I don't want to wrap up your life with my situation. Maybe we should just back off from one another for a little while."

"Mason..." She laughed and he immediately caught offense.

"Not feeling like being mocked right now. What the fuck is so funny?"

"I'm not letting you do that thing you do this time. If you think you can get from up under me by being an ass, try again."

"Listen, I'm a grown man. You can't *let* me do anything." He beeped out a slow driver.

"I know but you're also my boyfriend." She giggled.

"Again, I'm a grown man. Not a boy."

"Wow, you don't even play anymore. Somebody really taking your attention away from me."

Silence.

What does she want? He thought.

"I know you a man, Mason. And I'm still not letting you walk out. You have to stand by me like you promised. So, if you have a problem, *we* have a problem. Can we finally agree?"

"Again, now is not a good time."

By T. Styles

"That's life when you're in a relationship. Things happen and you deal with them as a couple."

In the moment he wondered how to shake her forever. The emotional heat she was bringing was difficult. "What if I don't want the same thing anymore?"

"Again, we deal with them as a couple."

"Dasher..."

"Say my name as much as you like. I'm not going anywhere." There was some noise in her background. "I'm not giving up on you, Mason. I think you're used to that and you need to understand with me things are different. I don't tuck tail and run at the first sign of trouble. Okay?"

"I'll talk to you later."

Although he wasn't in the mood to speak, he had to admit he liked her style. Most people would run when given the option, but she seemed intent on staying the course.

Still, there was work to be done.

When he pulled behind Minnesota's Aston at the address, she had given him, he looked around, slid out and walked cautiously to the vehicle. After all, with Tobias being dead he was certain that at some point he would have to face Bolero, even though he felt he had time.

Still, he needed to move carefully.

The moment he slipped in the backseat, behind Minnesota, he smelled iron. Within seconds his eyes focused on Myrio slumped in the passenger seat. He sighed. This was why she couldn't go into detail over the phone.

"What the fuck is going on with old boy?" He asked.

Splattered with blood, Minnesota was trembling. Her eyes were cherry red, and she looked like she was on the verge of breaking down. "I, I killed him."

"I see that shit, but what the fuck happened? The last time I saw you at the wedding, you seemed to be feeling this little nigga."

"I don't know why I did it." She threw her hands up. "I mean, we were talking, and he wouldn't stop saying the same things over and over again. And he wanted, he wanted, I mean..."

"Say it!"

"He wanted me to go against my father."

Mason frowned and sat back. "What you mean go against your father?"

By T. Styles

She turned her body to look at him. "At the wedding, I, I saw him shoot and kill Tobias. Myrio was with me. He suggested I step to Bolero about it, I guess like leverage and... I don't know." She looked down.

"You saw Banks that night?"

"Yes."

"Fuck." When Tobias was shot, Mason was certain they were alone in the backyard and now he felt like shit. After all, it meant he had been caught slipping. "I can't believe this shit."

"And I wasn't sure but I'm thinking that maybe he was going to try and tell Bolero even if I said no."

"So, you were going to go against Banks?" He glared.

"At first I...I was mad about...about...about the baby and stuff." She stuttered. "But betrayal? That's too much even for me."

Mason dragged two hands down his face. "I can tell you had feelings for old boy. But if it's true, that he wanted you to go against Banks, you did the right thing. You don't put no nigga over family. Ever!"

She wiped her tears away. "I know...but I feel so bad because, I mean, I don't know what to do with his body."

"Don't worry about that. You good."

After a call was made, for the next five minutes they were silent. Suddenly a navy-blue van pulled alongside her car.

"Wait right here." Mason hopped out and talked to the three men. From the inside she could see he was giving instructions and for some reason she was calmer already.

Returning back to the car he opened the driver's door and said, "Come with me. I'm gonna have your ride cleaned and taken back to the Wales Estate."

"Okay, but where we going?"

"Just trust me."

As they slipped into his car, she could see the men fussing about her vehicle. "What are they doing, Uncle Mason?"

"Listen, a lot is happening. For the moment all I want is to get you some place safe and cleaned up. After that I'll tell you everything you need to know."

She nodded as another flood of relaxation came over her. "Thank you. Thank you."

By T. Styles

"Let's get out of here."

He put the car in drive.

And as she looked at him from the passenger seat, she couldn't help but give him a big side hug. It was the first time they shared a sincere moment since he attempted to kill her when the war first began. But none of those battles mattered anymore. And with this powerful act, their bond was back intact.

It was a good thing too. Because she would need him for the next horror, he had to prepare her for.

LUXURIOUS SUITES

Minnesota sat on the closed toilet seat in the hotel room talking to her friend Nasty Natty on the phone.

"I don't know, girl." Minnesota said taking a deep breath. "But he's going to tell me something important and I'm afraid." She wiped her hair behind her ear.

"Like, what do you think he could possibly say? Because to be honest, you're making me nervous now."

Minnesota shook her head. Her friend was always extra, but it felt good talking to her again. It had been some time since their fall out but since they reconnected after Minnesota popped up over her house, they didn't miss a day without speaking. "It's not about you this time."

"True but still. I mean what if he's going to tell me my father knows I was about to betray him?"

"If he knew you wouldn't have had to tell him when he scooped you up. Nah...I really think it's something else, Minnesota. Maybe he wants to talk about the falling out you had with him."

"Why you say that?"

"Because, you've had issues with Mason before. But he seems to really want to help now and maybe he's using this time to clear the air. I could be wrong but—"

"That does make sense. We could hardly stand each other and now it's like...I don't know...being around him reminds me of Arlyndo."

"You miss him?"

"Sometimes I do." Minnesota sighed. "I guess I'm just running my mouth and—"

"Get out of the bathroom and go out there to see what that man wants. Just tell me whatever he says."

She giggled. "I will."

"Plus, you know I can also be there within ten minutes if shit kicks off. As a matter of fact, I'm coming anyway."

"Wait, you serious?"

"Uh, yeah. I want the details and I don't want the watered-down version of whatever you gonna give me."

Minnesota laughed. "You crazy."

"I'm on my way. But go see what Uncle Mason's fine ass wants now."

"I thought you said the Louisville's were dusty."

"They are. But they fine too."

"Bye, girl!" Minnesota took a deep breath and hung up.

When she walked into the room Mason was pacing by the door on the phone. Observing him in silence, she crossed her arms over her chest and leaned against the wall. "Uncle Mason."

He looked at her. "Hey."

"Sorry it took me so long in there."

He ended the call and said, "It's cool. Are you okay?"

She sighed deeply. "I guess it depends on whatever you're about to say. Because I can't tell if it's serious or not."

"It is very serious."

She swallowed the lump in her throat. "I'm listening."

"Your father's sick."

She dropped her arms at her sides and approached him. "What do you, what do you mean?"

He looked down and back at her. "I don't want to scare you unnecessarily."

"You've done that already."

"I know and I'm sorry. But I will tell you everything once we're there."

"Once we're where? Because earlier you said you would let me know when we got here."

"Everything will be clear soon. Where are your bloody clothes?"

"In the bathroom. In the bag you gave me."

"Go get 'em."

She ran into the bathroom. Grabbing the clothes that she was wearing she handed the bag to him. "Okay now what's up?"

"We're going to Jerseys estate."

"Okay." She felt lightheaded and afraid. "Uncle Mason, is my father alive?"

"Yes."

Some relief.

"But before we leave, I want to talk to you about something else. I never got a chance to say I'm sorry. You know, when things kicked off between you and I."

Natty was partially right.

"There's no reason to apologize."

He extended his palm in her direction. "Listen, I need to clear the air and get this off my heart."

"Oh, okay."

"I held you as a baby. I helped nurture you. And then when things got heated, I tried to take your life. Even though I knew Arlyndo...I mean...even though I knew how much you meant to my son. And I'm sorry for that."

She felt a swirl of emotion in her gut. "You really hurt me."

"I know. And I never got a chance to spend this time with you to be honest with how I felt. And, I mean, the way our family is dropping, I gotta, I gotta tell you where I'm coming from."

Minnesota didn't know how much she needed to hear those words until he uttered them.

Because quite honestly up until that moment she wasn't sure if he wouldn't finish what he started eventually. So instead of responding with words she rushed up to him and wrapped her arms around his body for the second time that day.

"Thank you so much for, for saying that."

When they separated, he said, "And now let's go. There's so much more to be said."

THE PETIT ESTATE
1972

Angela was in the attic, picking at the exposed pink fiberglass within the floor. When the door opened, fearing she would be poisoned again, she hid behind one of the pillars. When she saw her fourteen-year-old brother enter holding something behind his back, she slowly came into view.

"Hey..." he waved.

"Mother will get you for coming up here." She stepped in the middle of the attic, a bit closer, as he closed the door.

By T. Styles

"I don't care."

She tucked her hair behind her ear. "Well what do you want?"

He placed a pornographic magazine called 'Playboy' on the floor, along with a white sock stuffed with other socks so that it resembled a snake.

She glared. "Why did you bring that up here?"

"I hid it from mother."

"I asked why did you bring it here? To me?"

"Because...because it's yours."

Her white skin flushed red. "No, no it's not."

"Yes, it is." He smiled. "I saw you rubbing on it when you were in the bed. You like it a lot because when you do it you fall asleep. So, I—."

"That's a lie!"

He looked down. "No, it's not. I thought you liked it."

"I'm going to tell mother you were watching me in my room!" Angela said as she began to windmill his face and chest with tight fists.

Her blows left scratches about his face and arms, but she didn't care. She was about to do more harm until he ran out and locked the door behind himself.

When she was alone, embarrassed as fuck, she fell on the floor, with her forehead buried into her knees crying. Long slick silk strands ran from her nose as she wiped them away before lifting her head and taking a deep breath.

Sitting five feet away from the magazine and sock snake, she felt her heartrate increasing. Because Hercules was on to one big fact, the items did provide major relaxation.

Slowly she rose, grabbed the May 1971 magazine and the snake knot. Looking at the magazine, she sat carefully on the bed. On the cover was a blonde wearing a black latex scuba diving jacket. Her hair was wet, and she looked as if she'd been swimming. With the copy on the magazine being, 'Playboy's Scuba-Do'. The price for the magazine?

One dollar.

Angela would've paid a million if she could.

She idolized her so much, that she wanted to exude her sexuality.

Flipping the cover open, she quickly laid on her belly, stuffed the sock between her legs and rubbed herself slowly over the hump. The sensation was explosive and each time the knot ran over her button, she would tremble in ecstasy until she

By T. Styles

reached an orgasm. Over and over she would slide until she did it so many times, the sock was drenched with her oils and she was exhausted.

This would happen many times during the day, for weeks on end. It was the only thing, at the time, that kept her sane.

CHAPTER FIVE
DIAMOND HOTEL SUITES

Bolero was standing in front of the floor to ceiling window staring out at Baltimore City. He placed many calls after Spacey's wedding regarding the whereabouts of Tobias and he was starting to get livid due to no answers.

Things were about to get out of hand.

"I don't care that you've looked everywhere." He said in Spanish to one of his employees. "Because if you truly looked everywhere, he would be here. Now get out there and find out where he is."

"Yes, sir. Right away."

When he got off the phone with him, he made another call. Right before Mason picked up, he almost hung up. After all he'd called Mason's number more than twenty times to no avail. So, he was surprised he answered.

With his face clenched in a frown he said, "Where have you been?"

"Things—."

"Mason, where is Banks?" He said cutting him off. "And why haven't you answered in over twenty-four hours?"

By T. Styles

"We have a lot going on. But I'm answering now."

His jaw twitched. "So, this is how Banks treats a guest at a wedding? To not so much as say bye after I accepted his son's invitation?"

"Like you said, I didn't extend the invite. So, you have to talk to Banks about those matters."

Mason's tone was short and annoyed, and it didn't go unmissed. "Are you being disrespectful?"

"It's not—."

"Because I can cut you down where you stand. You do know that don't you? Or are you so foolish you don't realize who I am?"

"No need to make threats, Bolero. That can get ugly for everybody."

"Ugly for *everybody*?" He chuckled.

"That's what I said."

Bolero was dizzy with rage. The fact that Mason didn't respect the man he was, bothered him deeply. "Let me make myself clear, I'm not one of your friends." His accent was so thick Bolero's words were almost unrecognizable.

"True. You are no friend of mine."

"And because I'm not one of your friends, I don't mind doing whatever I must to stop your world as you know it."

Silence.

"Mason."

"Yes."

"Do you understand?"

"This isn't about respect, Bolero. This is about being unable to give you the information you're seeking."

"No, it's about confusion. And it's about feeling like something is off. Now where is Banks? There are shipments ready to be organized and disseminated."

"Even with Banks not being available at the moment, I'm still handling the pickups."

He glared. "Oh, are you?"

"Yes. Banks isn't always hands on. You know that." He yawned which angered Bolero even more. "But business will proceed. It always has and it always will."

Bolero walked to the other end of the window and tried to let the beautiful skyline calm his nerves. It wasn't working. One minute he was going to help Spacey celebrate his nuptials and the next the entire Wales Estate was being cleared out without a word.

"I'm surprised to hear you'll be handling shipments."

By T. Styles

"Why is that?"

"Because I spoke to Banks and he led me to believe that you were getting out of the game. Has this changed suddenly? Because I have to tell you, the way you and your friend handle matters sounds suspicious."

Silence.

"Mason, are you in or are you out?" He asked through clenched teeth. "Because I don't have time for games."

"I don't know where he could have gotten me being out the game. But Banks knows that if he's in the business, I'm in it for life."

"Well you had better clear that up with him."

"No need."

"I doubt that seriously."

"Sir, is there anything else?"

Bolero shuffled a little. "Where is Tobias?"

"Why you asking me?"

"Well, as you know we don't have the best of relationship, but he stays in contact when it comes to matters of business."

"I do."

"Well strangely enough, since the wedding I've been unable to find him. And I'm looking for answers."

"The last I saw he was at the ceremony with his girlfriend. Maybe you should talk to her."

"I did over the phone."

"She couldn't provide answers?"

"No."

"Well you should ask around a bit more. Because I'm lost."

"That also strikes me as odd. As you know I still have my ears to the streets. And everyone led me to believe that you and him developed quite the bond. So, if there was anyone on the planet to know where he is, I would think it would be you." He paused. "And the fact that you are pretending—"

"I'm not pretending."

"I'm not sure about that. It appears that I'm getting the runaround. So, let me make things clear, I expect Tobias to call me within the next few hours. And if he doesn't there will be problems."

"Again, maybe we should pause on the threats."

"No threat. This is a promise. Am I understood?"

Silence.

"Mason..."

"I got it."

Bolero hung up.

By T. Styles

"I hope you know he's lying." Cassandra said slyly in Spanish.

Bolero turned around and faced her. "What?"

"I mean, you can't possibly be that stupid to believe he doesn't know where my brother is. If I had to guess, I would say he's dead." She walked to the bar and poured herself a glass of recently opened red wine.

"Watch how you speak to me. Your ignorance can find you in a world of trouble. You know that."

"Maybe, but I'm not the one that's ignorant."

He was just about to slap her down when Roxana entered. "No need to be angry with my sister, father. She's right."

"Don't call me that." He glared.

She giggled. "Bolero, there's no need to be angry. Something is going on with the Wales'. We've seen it all before."

"You may have seen a few things but the way your mind is set up, I'm not sure if you're able to understand."

"You're right." Roxana added holding her stuffed animal. "I may be a little special. But that makes me see things better. And like I said, the Wales and the Lou's have made it clear they don't consider our lives worth protecting. We have been pawns in their games since we met them. And if they want to get rid of us that's exactly what they'll do. Unless you stop them."

"This is one of the reasons we can't develop a bond." He said. "You don't know your place. Either of you."

"Are you going to *finally* be a father and stand up for me?" Cassandra said. "Roxana? And Tobias? Or are you going to pretend we don't exist?"

"I will do things my way."

"Bolero, I'm here to see my brother." Cassandra continued. "I have come across oceans to do that. And I won't be leaving without answers. Whether you help me or not. That's all I'm saying."

Bolero looked at the two women who shared his bloodline. His peculiar relationship with them was definitely one for the books. On one hand he chose to pretend as if he wasn't their biological father. Because by doing so, he wouldn't have to admit that he slept with the love of his brother's life. And on the other hand, he felt a strong need to protect them. And so, Tobias going missing was almost like proclaiming war.

Bolero took a deep breath. "Now I have some errands to run. Keep your sister in this hotel room,

96

Cassandra. I don't want to have to look for both of you too." He walked out the room.

The moment he was gone Roxana rushed up to Cassandra. "So, what we waiting on?"

She flopped on the sofa. "What you talking about?"

"So that speech about crossing oceans to find Tobias was a lie?"

Cassandra grabbed a magazine and flipped a page. "Don't be stupid."

"He doesn't care about us." She sat next to her. "The only reason he does what he does is because our uncle would kill him from prison if something happened to us."

Cassandra shook her head. "Oh, you don't think I know who has the main power in this family? You really tripping now."

Roxana glared. "I'm not stupid, sister."

"You know that's not how I look at you."

"I can't tell. More importantly I don't care anyhow."

She tossed the magazine down. "Roxana, what are you saying?"

"I'm saying we need to find our brother on our own. Without Bolero's help."

"But we barely know where we are."

"We know where they live. We saw the place remember? For the wedding."

"And how do you propose we get there?"

"A cab." She shrugged. "Downstairs. There were lots of them."

Cassandra sighed deeply. "This feels like a bad idea."

"Maybe, but that's why we should do it even more."

Cassandra took a deep breath and stood up. "Okay, I'll go see what I can find out."

Roxana rose. "You? You can't possibly think I'll be staying in this room by myself ."

"Bolero says that you must—"

"I don't care what Bolero says. He's not my father, remember? Anyway, it was my idea." She moved toward the door. "Now you can stay in this room or come with me. Either way it makes me no difference."

CHAPTER SIX

Spacey was driving the car quickly with Derrick in the passenger seat while Jersey sat in the back with Shay. The tension was so thick that it made even sitting together uncomfortable. Every now and again Shay would look over at Jersey and smile, loving how much she glowed while pregnant despite the terrible atmosphere in the air.

"You look beautiful, Jersey." Shay said. "Are you wearing makeup?"

Jersey touched her cheeks, as if trying to remember if she found time to make herself look differently than she felt. "No. I don't...I don't think so."

"Wow, I can't tell." Shay looked at her skin closer and squinted. "It really looks like you beat your cheeks."

Jersey smiled for the first time all day. "That's good because I hate that I'm the most stressed I've ever been."

Shay looked at her belly and then at Derrick who was texting on his phone. "What does it feel like?"

Jersey frowned. "What you mean?"

"Like, to give life?" Shay shrugged. "I mean I always wondered what it meant to be pregnant. But...you know."

"You're still young. There's plenty of time."

Derrick, unable to take much more, turned around and looked back at his girl. "I don't know why you worried about all that shit. You ain't pregnant and you not going to get pregnant."

Shay frowned. He was notorious for greasing up the mood. "Nigga, I'm not talking to you."

In the backseat Jersey squeezed Shay's hand lightly and shook her head. The last thing she wanted was her son going off. "Please don't." She whispered to her.

She was about to calm down, but Derrick was ready for war. And so, he turned his entire body around as if he didn't have a good view already. "You don't have to be talking to me. I'm not about to have no baby with you. I done already told you that. So, calm the fuck down."

She crossed her arms over her body. "Well if you don't give me one, I'll find somebody else."

"Don't get fucked up."

"Cut it out," Spacey said to him.

"She be fucking with me, man." Derrick sat back in his seat. "Sometimes I don't even know why I deal with her."

"I know, but just chill." The car was awkwardly silent for a few minutes until Spacey said, "So, uh, why don't you like babies? If you ask most people on the planet, they would say babies are the only things universally loved."

"Well I ain't most people."

"Everybody already knows that shit, roach." Shay said rolling her eyes.

Derrick's skin felt hot to the touch. "Look, what ya'll not going to do is double team me because I'm my own man. And I'm not having no baby with her or nobody else. Period. So, stop bringing it up because my mind ain't changing."

Shay started laughing and shaking her head, knowing how to get at him.

He looked back at her. "What's funny?"

"You act like somebody want that raisin dick you toting."

"Whatever!"

"Yeah whatever! It amazes me how you're the one who muscled yourself into my conversation and then you wanna fake flex. I was talking to your mother and you all in mine."

"Because I don't want her filling your head with nonsense."

"I'm grown, Derrick."

"I hear all that, Shay, but babies ain't nothing but trouble."

"This nigga goofy." Shay added.

"It's true. They don't provide nothing to the world. Just pain. So, cut out all that noise."

He took a deep breath and everyone in the car suddenly knew where his issues originated. The Wales in the Louisville families were losing members like petals from flowers. And if any of them sat in silence for a moment, and thought about the lives lost, the pain would be too great to handle.

"It's a wonderful feeling." Jersey whispered to Shay quietly. "It's almost as if God has given you a specific duty. To bring hope into the world. I mean, I may be older, but I take childbirth very seriously. I'm just honored to be at my age and still be able to do it. Not everybody can say the same."

"Fuck, what did I just say, ma?" Derrick yelled. "Plus, ain't you got babies to deal with already?"

"Yes, Derrick. Your brothers."

"Where are they?" Spacey frowned realizing he hadn't seen them.

"Gina has them. I sent her a text earlier and she says everything's fine."

"Anyway, them little niggas not my brothers." Derrick continued. "Remember? No direct bloodline to you. So, stop all that noise."

"Dumbass, they are your brothers. Or did you forget that ya'll share the same father?" Shay reminded him.

Silence.

Spacey thought about his new wife who was devastated when he told her earlier that the honeymoon would be postponed. "Well I'm having a baby." He said proudly.

Up until that point it had been mostly a secret. But now since everyone was sharing, he felt it was his duty to let the news free. In fact, the only ones he told outside of Banks and Jersey was Minnesota when they shared a dance on the floor at his wedding reception.

Shay grabbed her cheeks in excitement. "Congratulations! I'm so happy for you. I wanna be the godmother."

He didn't know about all that but what he did say was, "Thank you. I appreciate it."

Derrick, more irritated than ever said, "Man, I need to get out of this car. Because I'm about to kill everybody in this bitch."

JERSEY'S ESTATE

Mason, Minnesota and Natty walked into Jersey's foyer. As he moved toward the back of the estate to check on Banks, they headed into the living room and sat on the sofa as he instructed.

Within five minutes he was back in the living room looking more stressed than ever. It was as if he aged ten years in minutes.

Sitting close to Natty, as she held onto her friend's hand, Minnesota asked, "What's going on, Uncle Mason?"

"As you know your father hasn't been well over the past few months."

"Okay..."

"It's gotten worse."

She shook her head and shrugged. "You mean the stress headaches, right?"

By T. Styles

"If that's what you call them. But to be honest nobody knows what they are. All we know is that he's been dealing with them a lot. And before he would pop a pill and be fine but that doesn't work anymore."

Minnesota shifted a little. "Okay, is...I mean...is my father—"

"Just listen, sweetheart."

Natty held Minnesota's hand tighter.

Right before he was about to explain in great detail the door opened and in rolled Jersey, Spacey, Derrick, and Shay.

"Uncle, Mason, where is Pops?" Spacey asked with a ball of anxious energy. "Jersey said something's wrong. I need to see him."

Minnesota stood up and her friend remained at her side. "Okay, now I'm really scared, Uncle Mason."

"Wait, you didn't tell Minnesota about pops yet?" Spacey asked. "Because she has the right to know."

"I was about to do that before ya'll came in." Mason took a deep breath and did his best not to go off on his pregnant ex-wife for bringing drama his way. It was bad enough he was suffering too. "Your father has a tumor in his head. And they're doing surgery right now in the bedroom to remove it."

Always one for the dramatics, Shay immediately took off running toward the back to see what was happening.

"Grab her ass!" Mason ordered. "Because if they botch up that surgery cause she starting shit, I'll kill her."

Immediately Derrick grabbed her by the waist and hoisted her back into the living room. It didn't matter that she was kicking and screaming. "Get off of me, nigga! Get off!"

"Calm down, stupid bitch!" Derrick said.

"Are you people fucking crazy?" Shay yelled looking at every one. "My father is in there about to die and we acting like everything fine?"

Nasty Natty was confused. "Not for nothing, but when did he become your father again?" She looked around for answers.

Shay glared at Natty. She remembered her from the past and couldn't stand her then or now. "So, you back on this bitch, Minnesota?"

"She's a friend."

"So, your friend picks now to question me about my family?" Shay continued. "I mean, didn't you school her?"

106   By T. Styles

"Shay, please cut it out." Minnesota said as tears rolled down her cheeks. "We have zero time for this shit."

"Yeah, relax." Derrick said. "We here to find out what the fuck is going on."

Shay looked around and immediately felt attacked. "I know what this is about." She pointed at all of them.

"Girl, what you talking about now?" Minnesota threw her hands up in the air.

"Ya'll never respected me as a member of this family."

"That's not true." Spacey said.

"It is! And the gag is I care more about that man than all of you put together." She pointed in the back. "And when he was having headaches, I was the one who checked on him. I was the one who made his load lighter. I cleaned his clothes when he couldn't get up. While all of ya'll were out living your lives."

Jersey frowned.

"You sound dumb!" Spacey said.

"What about when my Kirk was shanked in prison and died, and dad came home fucked up, where were all ya'll then? Huh? On the island living your lives."

The room went into a frenzy. Loud voices. Flailing arms. Wales Island was a nightmare and all present knew it was true. Besides, there was no one in that room that believe they cared more about Banks than themselves, and they wanted her to know.

"Listen...listen...!" Mason yelled.

Everyone was still yelling.

"I SAID SHUT THE FUCK UP!"

Slow silence.

With a deep breath he said, "Like I said, Banks is having surgery. And everybody in this room is welcomed to stay until we figure out what's going on. But if you stay, if you remain, you will be quiet, and you will be respectful. Or you can get the fuck out. Your choice."

"Well that's kind of you considering this is my house." Jersey said sarcastically rubbing her belly. "That *my* fiancé bought for *me*."

Mason folded his arms to prevent from stealing her in the jaw. "All I'm saying is if you're staying, today, we don't need agitated energy. Because I'm not sure what's going on in that room." He placed a hand over his heart. "But the doctors are trying their best to save his life. And I need them to do just that."

By T. Styles

Queen of making it about her said, "Everybody hates me!" She took off running down the hallway. Since it was in the opposite direction of where Banks was having surgery no one but Derrick and Nasty Natty followed.

When Shay made it to the back of the large estate, she bunkered down in a small guest bathroom within the basement. Once inside she closed and locked the door, before crying heavily.

Derrick and Natty walked up to the door.

"Wow, is she going to be okay?" She whispered.

He sighed deeply. "I, mean, for real, I don't know what's going on right now. She been gaining weight, acting crazy and I'm sick of it."

She sighed. "Well, how are you?"

He scratched his head. "I hadn't really thought about it for real."

"You should. Because I don't know your relationship with Banks, but a lot is happening. Especially since your father loves him so much. Take care of yourself too."

He nodded. "Everybody bugging right now."

"Well I'm here if you need to talk."

Truth be told everyone knew she always had a crush on the Louisville boys. Although they were grungier than the Wales family, there was nothing that could be said bad about their looks. Which she always appreciated.

He ran his hand down his face. "I want this day over. Quick."

"Worried about your girl?"

"Not really. She gonna be okay." He said as he sat on the floor next to the door. "She just acting out like always."

She smiled and sat next to him. "Well I'm gonna stick here with you." She whispered.

He smiled and nodded slowly. "Okay by me."

CRYSTAL SUITES

Gary, Nidia's right-hand man was pacing the floor inside of the hotel room he rented in Washington D.C. He had been calling Myrio

By T. Styles

nonstop, and yet all of his calls had gone unanswered.

It fucked him up because at one point everything seemed to be going smoothly. With Myrio's assistance, originally the plan was to get to Minnesota so that they could access the shipment of quality cocaine Bolero provided. After all, since Nidia was gone, the streets were dry and so he needed Myrio with his good looks to get to the Plug's daughter.

And he had done just that.

Until her nerves were so bad that she accidentally killed him. Something that Gary was unaware of at the moment.

After he hung up the phone and sat back into the sofa within the suite he sighed deeply. "This doesn't look good."

"Still no word on the boy?" Christopher asked, going over to the bar to pour two glasses of vodka.

"No."

"You don't think they found out about our plan, do you?" He walked over and handed him one glass. "Banks and them?"

"I hate to say it, but I'm starting to think that's exactly what happened." He drank half. "Why else wouldn't Myrio answer my calls?"

"Fuck, it seems like everybody who deals with this family ends up dead." He sat next to him.

Gary thought about what he said. He thought about Nidia being murdered and he thought about how everyone who crossed a Wales or Louisville member ended up missing. He was right.

"I'm sick of the Wales and the Lou's."

"So, what you wanna do?" Christopher asked taking another sip.

"Before the day ends, I want them all dead. Even if I have to do it myself."

CHAPTER SEVEN
JERSEY'S ESTATE

Jersey sat at her kitchen table looking out the window. The sun was shining inside and appeared to make the yellow chiffon curtains glow. She was searching for one ounce of relief. And so, she made herself a pot of decaffeinated English tea. She was about to cry when Spacey walked inside.

"I didn't know you were in here."

"Yeah, just wanted to, you know."

"I get it. I feel like I'm coming down with something. Throat is kind of sore. Wanted to grab something to drink. "

For a moment she rubbed her belly, concerned of giving a cold to her baby. "I hope you're okay."

"I'm fine." He breathed deeply. "The kettle still hot?"

She nodded.

"Mind if I pour a cup?"

She moved uneasily. Normally she would not spend any alone time with him, so the moment was awkward. "Of course not. Join me."

Spacey poured himself a cup, pulled out the chair and sat in front of her. "This is a really nice spot. The house. You guys went all out didn't you?" He took a sip.

"I can't take any credit. Banks built it for me."

He nodded. "Not surprised. My father has taste." He took a deep sip as he tried to erase the thought of losing him. "So, um, how have you been?"

She laughed.

"What's funny?"

"I don't know." She shook her head. "I'm tired of people asking me how I am as if being pregnant is a disease."

He placed his cup down. "I actually didn't mean it that way. I'm talking about how are you mentally? Since we have all of this going on. It has nothing to do directly with your baby."

She moved uneasily in her seat. Since she judged him incorrectly, she was forced to eat her words. "I'm sorry, Spacey. Things have been so crazy that I guess I'm a little defensive at times."

He nodded. "Understood. But why?"

"Because I don't believe people are giving me the respect they would, let's say, your mother. Every time I ask how he's doing, to Mason or even Preach, it's like I'm bothering them or something."

He shrugged. "Maybe they aren't giving you respect because you don't deserve it. Let's be real, you sleeping with my mother's husband. And as far as I remember, she was your friend."

"That's not fair!"

"It's true. I don't say much because I want my father happy. And after my mother's death you appeared to do that for him. But let's be clear, I don't think how you went about shit was right. I mean, we needed time to heal."

"I'm not the one who did this first, Spacey. And although I can see how it's easy to blame me, if your mother hadn't did what she did with Mason, we wouldn't have been in this situation."

"I give you that. My mother and Mason were wrong too. But everybody in this room knows you took it an extra step with being in a relationship."

Jersey felt dizzy.

"Maybe you're right. I guess I couldn't see past who I wanted. I mean I know he is your father but to me he was my hero. My savior. And I wasn't willing to compromise that feeling just because people don't understand our bond. And I'm not willing to compromise now."

"That makes you selfish."

"Selfish?"

"You want me to say it again? Because I can if you didn't hear me the first time." He took another sip.

She shook her head. "You know, this world is so fucking strange."

He pushed back in his chair and poured himself another cup. "Oh yeah, tell me about it, Mrs. *Louisville*."

"I'm serious. People want you to apologize for things you aren't sorry for. It's like hearing the words will make them feel better about not going after what or who they want in life. But I'm not sorry, Spacey. I love Banks. I love him more than I loved anybody."

"Including Mason?"

"Yes. *Especially* after being with Mason. Because it's only through seeing how a good man treats you that you realize the other man wasn't about shit. And if you or anybody else wants to blame me for my heart, then so be it."

"Jersey, I didn't mean it like—

"You meant what you said." She stood up. "Remember, no fake apologies. Enjoy the rest of the tea that I made, nigga. Because It'll be the last thing I do for your ass. Ever." She got up and walked away.

By T. Styles

Nasty Natty was in the bar within Jersey's estate drinking Hennessy with ice when Derrick strolled inside. Immediately she fiddled with her hair, in an attempt to make herself look more presentable.

He winked and poured himself a large cup of Hennessy as he flopped in the seat next to her.

"Thirsty much?" She asked.

"Very." He cleared his throat. "I forgot to say I'm surprised you're here. To support whatever's going on with Banks."

"Nope, it's really me." She giggled. "And I'm really here."

He nodded and took a sip before burping.

"Hold up..." She crossed her legs. "Why you so shocked? Is it because Banks almost killed me?"

"Pretty much."

"I guess it's 'cause I know it wasn't done on purpose. And from what he said when he brought me money—."

"He gave you cash?"

"Yep. Over a million. After that, I realized he was just trying to find Minnesota. And that the people he hired reacted too harshly."

"You believed him?"

"I had no choice."

He took a large sip. "Let me ask you something."

"Shoot."

"The real reason you're back in Minnesota's life is not to get revenge is it?" He frowned. "Because that's the last thing this family needs right now."

She leaned her head back. "And here I was beginning to think that you hated the Wales Family. Let me find out you have a change of heart."

"Nah, I despise them. They've taken everything from me. And I'm pretty sure Banks had something to do with Howard going missing."

"Wow."

"Trust me, I earned the right to hate them. And at the same time...at the same time...I'm in a situation where you can't pick and choose your family. Because God knows I tried." He shrugged.

"I get it. You're like me. At the end of the day I'm here because I fuck with Minnesota. We were

By T. Styles

really close at one point and we will continue to be close no matter what happens."

"That's good to hear."

She turned her entire body toward him. "Okay, now it's my turn. Are you really into Shay? I mean for real, for real?" She threw a hand up. "She's ratchet. Loud. Disrespectful."

"I'm a Louisville nigga. That's my speed."

"But she's a mess, Derrick."

"Says the woman whose nickname is Nasty Natty."

She giggled. "There's a reason I have my name. And it ain't got shit to do with my attitude." She licked her lips. "And I know you already know that too."

"You still talk a lot of shit. After all this time."

"That will never change." She licked her lips again. "Don't let the time between us fool you. I'm still the same bitch." She stared at him a bit longer than she should have.

"Why you looking at me like that, girl?"

"Derrick, don't play games. You and me both been there before with each other. Like I said, it's still me. I just have a little limp after getting shot that's all."

"And I think that bop's sexy too."

Just then Minnesota walked inside. It was a good thing because they were vibing hard. "Derrick, you need to go see about Shay. She's still in that bathroom crying."

He sighed deeply. "She gonna be okay."

"Derrick!" Minnesota said louder. "Go check on your bitch."

He rolled his eyes. "I swear that girl's getting on my fucking nerves." He stood up and moved toward the door.

When he was gone, Minnesota shook her head and sighed. "What you drinking, Natty?"

"What I always drink?"

"You mean honeyed piss?" Minnesota sat across from her.

Natty laughed. "Don't play with me. You know I enjoys my drank."

Minnesota smiled and took a deep breath. "I just want this day to be over. Like, all this shit crazy."

"It is." She nodded.

Minnesota was beating around the bush and avoiding what she really wanted to talk about. "Don't let Derrick wrap you up again."

"Minnie, I'm just—."

By T. Styles

"Minnesota." She said correcting her. "You know I don't go by that shit no more. I'm a grown ass woman."

"Okay, well, *Minnesota*, I'm just here to support you." She sipped her drink. "I ain't here for nothing else."

"And I appreciate that. For real. It's just that, well, I don't want to go through what we went through before."

Natty frowned. "And like I said, ain't nobody thinking 'bout Derrick's ass. You gonna have to trust me."

"You think I didn't know ya'll were fucking before? You don't remember me catching him bending you over on my bed, when we had that cookout at my house?"

She didn't.

"You don't think I know him dumping you was the reason you tried to kill yourself that time?"

"Don't go—"

"That shit's dead." She said cutting her off. "Dead, Natty. He's with my sister now. So, back off."

Natty laughed." I can't believe you calling that bitch your sister. She doesn't have the Wales blood. I mean let's be real."

"True, but my brother loved her before he was killed. And I love you. But Shay is family. And if you want to be in my life you have to respect their bond."

Jersey was in her tub taking a quick bath. Since she was so late in her pregnancy, she found it harder to hold water. And so, after beefing with Spacey she urinated on herself unexpectedly in the hallway.

Just sitting in her own tub and relaxing brought back memories. She thought about the nights she and Banks would run a tub, hit the jets and talk for hours about love and life. Granted, he never took off his boxers, but she still felt special that he shared those precious moments with her.

When she felt herself about to cry, she took a deep breath. "Pull yourself together, Jersey. Banks is alive. Calm down."

When she attempted to get out of the tub, she suddenly discovered she was having a hard time. She was so caught up into wanting to relax and get clean that she didn't consider that every muscle on her body felt incapable of moving.

Luckily, she had her phone near because she was playing music. She needed assistance. Dialing a number, she waited for help.

A few minutes later Mason knocked on the door. "Jersey, you want me to come inside?"

Embarrassed beyond belief, she took a deep breath. This was the worst-case scenario. "Please. It should be unlocked."

He opened the door and tried not to focus on her very naked, very pregnant body. "What you need me to do?"

"Can you hand me that towel over there?"

He looked around, spotted the strawberry colored towel and did as she requested. "What else you need?"

"Uh, this is a bit awkward, but can you help me out?"

"Help you out with what?"

"Can you help me out of the tub, Mason. I'm literally having a hard time maneuvering my stomach and getting out at the same time."

He looked at her for a moment.

She looked at him.

And suddenly they busted out laughing. It was a genuine laughter reflective of one of those rare moments they shared when they were married, and things were good.

And that quickly it dissipated.

He felt guilty for his happiness since his friend was possibly dying. So, he cleared his throat and walked deeper inside. "Yeah, give me a second."

Moving closer to the tub, he reached over her body and lifted her out by holding her waist. His thumbs were inches from her swollen breasts as her arms wrapped around his neck.

"Don't worry, I got you." He said. "I won't let you go."

For a moment their flesh connected, and they looked into each other's eyes. "Thank you...thank you."

An emotional mess and needing a human connection, within seconds her face moved forward, preparing for a kiss until he pushed her softly away. "What you...what you doing?"

The towel dropped in the water. "I was just wanting to—."

"Let me make myself clear, what we have is done, Jersey. And while my man is back there fighting for his life the last thing, I'm gonna do is

By T. Styles

disrespect this whatever the fuck situation ya'll have together."

"I didn't mean it that way."

"It's done." He assisted her out of the tub and walked out.

Feeling stupid and embarrassed, she sat on the closed toilet seat and cried softly.

JERSEY'S ESTATE

Everyone in the household stood next to the door when Preach and the doctors walked out. Having been in the room all day, the medical staff looked exhausted and drained. Neither the Louisville's, Wales' nor Natty felt they had the look of confidence.

And that scared them.

Quincy stepped up and took a deep breath. "We did what we could, and unfortunately—."

Before the doctor could finish talking Mason stole him in the face and released his weapon from his waist band ready to take his life. Aiming in

Quincy's direction, it was Preach who stopped him from going too far by removing it from his grasp.

"Let him finish!" Preach yelled.

The doctor held his throbbing bloody lip and looked at his fingertips. "I was going to say unfortunately we can't tell what's going on until the next couple of hours. But we are keeping a close eye on things."

Everybody gasped in relief. Because although he hadn't given them the validation that Banks would be fine, in the moment, at least he was alive.

"Well why the fuck would you say it like that?" Mason asked as Preach handed him back his gun. He tucked it in his waist. "You know niggas tense and shit."

"You didn't let me finish." Quincy continued.

"Yeah, but you should've got right to the point." Spacey said.

Quincy frowned. "And you are?"

"It don't matter who he is, nigga." Derrick said. "Do your fucking job."

Quincy rolled his eyes.

"Listen, I don't know what type of game you on but I'm serious..." Mason said. "If my friend dies you die too. And that's on mothers."

Rev sat on the bed talking to Banana on the phone. When she coughed, he shook his head because this was the effect he didn't want. "I knew I shouldn't have let you take care of me."

"I'll be fine." She coughed again. "The last thing I need is you worrying about me. How are things over—."

The door opened just as he coughed into his hand.

It was Mason. He closed the door behind himself.

"Hey, Banana I gotta hit you back. Get some soup and rest, okay?"

"Sure will...and I'll see you soon."

Rev tossed his phone on the bed and Mason shook his hand.

"How you holding up?"

"I'm fine. A little fever or whatever. Something slight." Rev shrugged. "What's going on with Banks?"

Mason sighed and wiped a hand down his face. "It's not looking good, man. At all."

Rev sighed. "Listen, I know you think this will be the end but—."

"Before you finish, I know you about to say something positive. And I'm—."

"I'm in my sixties, Mason." Rev said raising his hand. "Whenever I talk its wisdom, not positivity. Don't confuse the two as being the same."

Mason took a deep breath. "My bad."

"What I wanted to say is simple...all of the energy, every thought you have, has to be focused on one small fact. You can't change what *needs* to happen."

"So, you saying if Banks dies it's supposed to go down?" He asked angrily.

"I'm saying that every one of you need to consider what having Banks around meant. Think about how much you relied on him instead of living your own lives. And how you need to grow with the possibility of not having him around. That goes for you, Jersey and his kids."

"This shit hard."

"I know it is." He coughed. "Now I still don't believe it's his time to go. But if it is..." he tried to prevent choking up. "If it is his time to go, we all gotta accept it and be glad we knew a great man."

By T. Styles

CHAPTER EIGHT
THE PETIT ESTATE
1972

*A*ngela looked down at her clothing repeatedly. Although she was only released once a day to dress and shower, she made sure to pick clothing that her mother would approve. That included dresses past her knees. Long sleeve shirts. No cleavage tops and long socks.

It was important to put on the best face in the hopes that her mother would let her out of the garret. Something it seemed she was far from doing.

When the door opened Gina walked inside, with an air of seriousness. She was holding a brown paper bag that was rolled tightly. From the way things moved around inside, she could tell it wasn't food.

Grabbing a chair from the corner she took a seat. "Sit down. We must talk."

Quickly she obeyed and planted a weird smile on her face as she propped her body in the chair. "Okay, Mother."

Gina's head rose as if she were studying her daughter closely. "Well, how are you making out up here?"

She wanted desperately to say she desired to leave. "I'm fine."

"Are you?"

"Yes, and I love looking at our garden. It seems like the flowers open up a bit more when the sun comes out. As if they're dancing for me. I always dance back."

Gina frowned.

She sounded stupid.

Angela realized at that moment she went too far. "I dance in my mind I mean."

Gina wiped her thinning blond hair from her face. "Dinner is almost ready."

Angela nodded, worried about being poisoned but needing sustenance. "That's, that's good."

"I'll bring it up later." Gina changed her crossed legs to the other side. "I want to talk to you about something. And I want you to be honest."

Angela's eyes widened. Perhaps this could be the way she would be released. "Okay, Mother, you know I always want to be honest with you."

"Wanting to be honest and being honest are two totally different things."

By T. Styles

She nodded. "Of, of course. I...I get it."

Don't say the wrong things, Angela. Be very, very careful. This is definitely a test.

"Are you sexually active?"

Angela's eyebrows rose. "I don't understand what you're asking."

"But you do though. Besides, the question was straight forward, and I expect a straight answer. Are you having sex?"

Angela got up and walked toward the window. Her heart beat heavily, and she felt faint.

"Sit down."

Slowly Angela crept back to her seat. With her legs pinned together tightly she said, "I don't have sex."

"Are you sure?"

She nodded yes. "But, I mean, I do look at books sometimes." She looked down.

"Okay, now we're getting somewhere. What kind of books?"

"The ones I found under daddy's side of the bed."

Gina's face flushed red. "So, this is what you do now? Lie on your own father? The very man who begged me to let you back into our lives?"

"I'm not lying."

"You have to be. Because you didn't find anything pornographic in our room." She crossed her arms tightly. *"And this is just another example of how you want to manipulate this family."*

"I did find them there, mother. I found them and then took them. But other than that, I have never experienced sex. All I want to do is be a good young lady like you always wanted. Like how I looked on the box."

Gina continued to glare. *"I believe you're sexually active and—"*

"Why do you do this? Why, why do you say things that aren't true when it comes to me?"

Gina smiled, finally having taken her out of the calmness she seemed to possess. *"It's simple. I believe your heightened sense of sexuality is the reason you've been having problems. Perhaps if you weren't such a loose body, you wouldn't be losing your mind and expressing yourself frantically in public."*

Angela trembled. *"Mother, I always try my best to be right for you. I don't talk to boys. I barely have any friends. But it seems like nothing I do works. Almost like you're trying to find a reason to keep me here."*

"Stop being melodramatic."

132 *By T. Styles*

"Are you trying to keep me here, mother? Am I locked up?"

"Of course not! It breaks my heart that my only daughter has to be here. And at the same time, I don't trust you with yourself. Keeping you here, away from everything else, is just another way of keeping you alive."

Angela looked down at her twiddling fingers. "Mother, if it's true, can I leave?"

"Not now."

Angela nodded her head. "Of course."

"I need to make sure you aren't a danger to yourself. And I know you don't believe me, but this really is for your own good."

"Once I'm free you'll never see me again." She whispered.

"What did you just say?"

"Nothing." She took a deep breath. "It gets dark here. Really dark. Even with a light on. I don't like it here. Please. Let me out."

"I would've considered it, but the problem is you still lie to me. And as a result, I don't trust you." Gina picked up the paper bag and pulled out a pair of pink lace panties. "If you aren't having sex where did these come from? Everything I buy you is cotton. Did some strange man give you these?"

Angela shook her head slowly from left to right.

"Answer me." Gina pounded a fist into her palm.

Angela's body vibrated. "I don't want to be a part of this. I, I mean—."

"I won't ask you again. Where did these come from?"

She crossed her arms over her body and then let them fall at her sides. "I found them in daddy's car."

Gina dropped the underwear and they floated to the floor. "That's another lie!"

"I didn't want to tell you because I knew you would be angry with me. But that's exactly where I found them."

Slowly Gina rose. Taking a deep breath, she said, "I'll bring your meal soon. You should eat every bite to keep your strength up. But you will remain here until you learn to tell the truth."

She walked out.

When the door closed, she fell on the floor weeping. It was the hardest cry she had in a while. She was tiring of wondering if she was good enough. She was tired of trying to determine what her mother wanted. And at the same time, she realized she had better figure out what Gina desired soon if she wanted to get out of the garret.

By T. Styles

Remembering the book she stole from her mother's bedside, she removed it from her secret hiding place in a wooden panel by the window. It was there with her sock and porno book. Sitting down, she flipped the cover open.

The first page shocked her.

Brainwashing is an act of love. If done properly, you will possess the undying loyalty of whoever you mean to control. Let's begin.

Curious, she flipped through the table of contents. She scanned every word, pause and syllable. Her entire attention was focused on each page, as if they held the clue to what her mother wanted.

She was deep into the first chapter when she heard a lawnmower outside. Dropping the book, she quickly rose. Standing by the window, warm palms planted on the pane, she smiled at the stranger outside hard at work.

He was her age.

Wearing jeans with no shirt, his skin was brown, like desert sand. As he shoved the lawnmower a smile dressed his face as he nodded while singing. His happiness, although small, made her grin with delight. She'd never been around a black guy, as her part of town didn't have many. Even the hired help in the neighborhood were normally white and so she found him...well...exotic.

When he began dancing, she blurted out a laugh as she was enthralled with how much he enjoyed himself with such a mundane chore. How she wished she could do the same and yet her life appeared to be on a road filled with despair.

She was just about to open the window wider when he suddenly looked up at her. Almost as if he could feel her staring down at him.

"Hey beautiful!" He waved.

Embarrassed, she quickly sat down and pulled her knees toward her chest as a smile spread across her face.

Whether he knew it or not, he saved her life.

By T. Styles

CHAPTER NINE
THE PETIT ESTATE

Gina looked down at her great-grandsons Ace and Walid who were sleeping in their beds when Marshall walked into the room. She knew what he wanted to discuss and yet she wasn't in the mood.

Touching Walid's face, when his eyes opened, he appeared to glare her way. "Don't ask, Marshall."

"Gina, when are we going to have a conversation without you cutting me down? I may be young but I'm still a man. Or are you so rich that you believe my feelings are beneath you?"

She sighed deeply and sat on the dusty loveseat. "If you must waste my time on matters less important, go ahead." She threw her hand up. "You have the floor."

He crossed his arms over his chest. "Okay, well, I want to leave. To visit my family in Mexico."

Her jaw dropped although she quickly picked it back up. She hadn't expected his request. "So, you would leave me at this time? When I need you the most?"

His eyes widened with hope. "So, so you *need* me?"

"Not really but I like your company all the same."

He breathed deeply. "If I don't go home now, I never will."

"In case you aren't paying attention, I'm taking care of two babies. And there is much to be done in our home. I can't have you gone at this time. I'm sorry."

"Taking care of the babies is your choice. Not mine." He looked over at the beds where Walid was sitting up...watching.

"And you wonder why I never consider you to be my right hand." She pointed at him. "I want you to remember this moment because at the end of the day, when times get rough, this is when it counts."

"And still I must go."

She wanted to scratch out his eyes, cut off his head and spit down his throat. And still she knew something else was going on that he wasn't telling her about. "Who is she this time, Marshall?"

"Let's not go there."

"Or is it a he?"

He frowned. "What? Never."

138   *By T. Styles*

She laughed. "Please don't pretend that you don't go both ways. I found you up under a boy remember? And still I took you in, got you right and now look. Your entire world has changed, and you spite me still."

"You mean when you took me from my foster home and raised me as *your own?* In your garret? Because if you're talking about that moment then yes, I do remember. And for what you did to me you should be locked up."

"I didn't touch you until you were of age."

"But you groomed me very well didn't you? With the weird baths and massages?"

Silence.

"I'm leaving, Gina. This isn't up for debate."

She wanted to beg him to stay. But being able to control people with money forced compassion out of her heart. So, instead she said, "If you leave, I will not allow you back into my home. With what I have planned in the months to come, I need loyal people around. Very loyal people. I'm trying to save my family."

"So, you're disposing of me? Just because I want to go home?"

"On the contrary."

"So, you want me to choose you or my family?"

WAR 7: PINK COTTON   139

"I really don't think there's any other way. Who do you choose?"

He took a deep breath and walked over to the babies and smiled. Walid was glaring as if protecting his brother who was still asleep. "I can definitely see why you love them. They're perfect."

She nodded, secretly waiting for him to make a choice. "I know. And it's amazing how many of Angela's features they possess."

He turned to look at her. "Blood is blood. Even if it crosses ethnic lines."

Bringing him back on topic she said, "What are you going to do? Who are you going to choose?"

"I'm going to see my family in my country."

She glared. "Then get out of my face. Forever."

"Gina, don't—."

"Leave! And tell Hercules I need him now."

He looked at her for a few more seconds and took a deep breath. When he was gone, she cried silently.

Without sound.

Contrary to what some believed, crying inside was more painful than an audible one. Because the act of screaming itself provides relief a silent cry would never allow. She was definitely devastated.

By T. Styles

A few moments later Hercules entered. "What is it mother?"

She wiped her tears away. "Any word on Minnesota?"

"Are you ok?" He was concerned.

"Any word on Minnesota? Or Banks?" She said more firmly. Unwilling even at that moment to show emotion. "Or Spacey?"

He stood taller and raised his chin. "I've put out some feelers."

"And have they resulted in any findings? Because I've made clear that I need them located like yesterday."

"What about Joey?"

"I'm not interested in helping that drug addict."

He was so annoyed it was tough helping at all. "Mother, they chose the streets."

"True."

"And you have a larger plan. I know you do."

She glared. "Do you love having everything you desire?"

"Mother..."

"I asked you a very important question." She stood up and walked in front of him.

"I enjoy my lifestyle some. The money hasn't been the same, but I manage."

"Well prove it by putting eyes on them. And don't come back until you do. Otherwise, I won't have any use for you."

Z'S MANSION

The young woman stood in front of Z trembling. She knew what kind of man he was, and she needed to be perfect if her life was going to change for the better as did the lives of Kacie, a short white girl with ginger colored hair and Jasmine, a cute black girl with bohemian locs. Samantha had seen their lives rise up from the ashes to owning their own salons, which were nothing more than a front for cleaning money. And she wanted in.

At the same time, there were different girls who were hired to do different jobs. Only after proving yourself as a good prostitute were you given another responsibility. So, she had a long way to go.

"You're still overweight." Z said plainly looking at her flesh. A towel hung over his shoulder. "And you aren't toned enough."

"I know, and I'm sorry." Samantha said clearing her throat. "I, I guess it's been a rough few days."

Kacie rolled her eyes. "I knew you'd be a problem. I should've never given you a chance."

"If you knew why you bring her to Z?" Jasmine asked crossing her arms over her chest.

"Obviously I wanted to give her the benefit of the doubt." She looked at Samantha again. "I guess I was wrong."

"Get on the table." Z instructed. "Legs up."

Samantha eased on the dining room table and removed her tights, followed by her panties. Opening her legs, she showed the recent labiaplasty he ordered from his surgeon. "Well, at least that looks good. The men will—"

The doorbell chimed.

"Stay here." Z said wiping his hand off a towel and throwing it on her belly. "I'll be back."

Walking to the door he was surprised when he opened it, only to see Gary, flanked by four men on each side. Immediately he grew nervous knowing that if he was there, it meant trouble was near. "Please, please, come in."

Following Z, they walked past the white girl on the table and into the living room. "Can I get you all anything to drink?"

Gary raised his hand no and pointed behind him. "I see you're one for flair as usual."

Slightly embarrassed about the girl sitting on the table Z shrugged. "It's business."

"I see." Gary nodded. "So, where is Myrio?"

Z frowned. "Myrio?"

"Don't repeat what I asked. Where is he?"

Z shook his head several times. "I, I don't know. The last I heard he was with the Wales girl." He snapped his fingers and pointed at him. "Minnesota, I think."

His comment reaffirmed what he already believed. "And when was that? That you talked to him last?"

"It was a while ago. Um, last night. He went to the wedding at the Wales house."

Gary looked at his men and back at Z, before taking a deep breath. "We had plans. If something happened to him I—."

"You want me to move on the streets? Give the word and I'll get answers. I know a few people he roll with from time to time."

"No. Keep things quiet. But I'm going to the Wales estate to see if I can get some answers first. I'll keep you in the loop. Stay assessible. I may need you tonight."

"No doubt."

Fifteen minutes later, Gary was in one of six vans headed to the Wales mansion. He was loaded with firepower eager to get revenge.

"Do you trust him?" Christopher asked sitting next to him in the back. "Z?"

"I do."

He nodded. "He would have no reason to lie. From what I understand, him and Myrio were doing quite well with the joy clubs."

"Exactly. But it's too soon to make any decisions about anything. We have to go see for ourselves."

Bolero was irritated.

He called Tobias a million times followed by hitting up Banks' phone and still he didn't get answers. And so, he decided to visit Tobias' girlfriend in the flesh.

"Like I told you on the phone, I was at the wedding, and, and, he was called out of the reception." Alexis cried as she stood in a robe, in her apartment. She was surrounded by Bolero and his men, and all meant business. "And he—."

"Called out by who?" Bolero said firmly.

"Um...I don't know..." She looked around, trying to rack her brain. But it was hard, mainly because she hadn't been with him long and didn't know a lot of the people in the Wales or Lou circles. Also, one of them seemed eager to shoot her in the face. "I can't remember."

He shook. "Think!"

Trembling, she searched harder. And then, as if the fog was cleared from the window she remembered. "The groom! He called him out when

By T. Styles

he was talking to us. Said someone wanted to speak to him in private."

Bolero stepped back. "Spacey Wales?"

"Yes! That's him."

Bolero glared.

"Thank you, young lady."

Fifteen minutes later he was back in his car being chauffeured by his bodyguard. He called his most trusted man. "I just left the girl. Where are you?" He asked Zeus Martin.

"I'm waiting for you, sir."

Looking out of the window he asked the question he already had an answer to. "Have you heard from Tobias?"

"No but I've put the word out that we've been looking for him."

His son was dead he was certain now. "And what you been hearing?"

"The same. That the last time anybody seen him was at the Wales wedding. I'm really starting to believe there's a connection."

Bolero did too. "Don't jump to conclusions."

"I'm trying not to. But at this point we can't deny the facts."

He knew his employee was being honest, and at the same time Banks and Mason brought big business his way. So, starting a war was a permanent and serious decision.

"What you want me to do, sir?"

"There's nothing left to do but to head to the Wales Estate. And this time we wait."

"I'm on my way."

By T. Styles

CHAPTER TEN
JERSEY'S ESTATE

Jersey leaned against the wall, in the living room. Her cell phone was pinned against her ear before she yanked it away and dialed another number. In the earlier part of the day, she had been in constant contact with the nanny, Gina. But now, it was as if she were ignoring her altogether.

With a glass of whiskey in hand for his nerves, when Mason saw the frantic look on her face, he approached. "What's going on now? The baby okay?"

"Yeah, uh, it's the twins. I've been trying to reach Gina for an hour with no response. When all this happened with Banks, she was talking to me but now..."

"Wait, you talked to her on the phone?" He was surprised because to be honest, he hadn't thought about hitting her phone when he first got the news she had taken the boys.

Now he felt dumb.

"Come with me."

He led her to the living room, and they sat on the sofa. So much was happening that he forgot to tell her about the babies. It wasn't that he didn't care. After all, Ace and Walid were his flesh and blood. But despite giving them birth, she had no real ties. Still, at the moment he felt it best to give her some clarity.

Sitting his glass on the floor he said, "I have to tell you something."

She braced herself by rubbing her belly. "Okay, well what is it? Because I've seen that look on your face before."

"I'll say it like this, their grandmother has them."

"What you talking about? Banks' mother is dead, and I don't deal with my—."

"First off their bloodline runs through me and Banks. So that's not what I mean."

Her jaw twitched. "Mason, where are *my* sons?" She stood up.

"Gina is their great-grandmother. And I don't have a lot of information but apparently, she's been involved in more ways than one in setting some foul moves from behind. Her motives aren't all the way clear though."

She frowned as the room began to spin. "I don't get it. I met her at a fertility appointment when—."

"I get all of that, Jersey. But you let a snake in our camp."

"How...how?"

"She been watching you from afar. She even had everything to do with my sperm being used. Yes, I gave it to her, but she was the one who let me on to what was happening. So, now they're with her until we locate this family."

She rubbed her throbbing head. "Why aren't you mad?"

"Jersey!"

"So, you're okay with this?" She asked throwing her hands up. "Because that's how you acting."

"Of course, I'm not okay with this shit. I have people looking for them as we speak. But with everything going on I really do believe it's best for them to stay with her. For today anyway."

Jersey felt ill. "But she's a complete stranger."

"Not necessarily. She has taken care of the boys since they were born, Jersey. She knows them like the front and back of her hand. Like I said, don't get it twisted, I have no intentions on letting my sons stay with her but right now the focus is on Banks."

Jersey almost fell until Mason helped her back to a seat. "I really don't understand what's going on in my life." She was talking mainly to herself. "And at the same time, I'm starting to believe a lot of this is our fault." She paused. "Seriously, what...what kind of life can be born from selling drugs?"

This was the last thing Mason felt like hearing. "One thing doesn't have anything to do with the other."

"But it does though, Mason. That's my point. We're in a situation where wc make money based off of people's weaknesses."

"Jersey...not this shit again."

"And yet we sit around and act like our lives should be okay. Like we deserve happiness, love and safety."

"You bringing me down. This not on my mind right now."

"It never is." She sighed deeply. "I don't know what plans you have to find the boys. But I want you to realize there's no way on Earth I'll allow her to keep them. I know they aren't my flesh and blood, but I still gave birth to them. Which makes me their mother. Even if you and Banks are unclear on the rest."

"I never said you weren't their mother. The three of us had everything to do with Ace and Walid being born. That much is true. And it's also true that there's no way on Earth that *I* will let her keep them either."

She breathed deeply. "As long as we're clear. I'm having a little girl in a few days. And I don't want her stressed out."

She stood up and he rose too.

"You good?"

Something was wrong. She clenched her belly. "No...I...I don't feel well."

"I'm gonna have Preach get in contact with the people at the birthing center. You use the same one right?"

She nodded yes.

"I'll make the call."

Normally she would fight harder, but she didn't have the energy. She was certain that she would be due any hour now. "I guess there's nothing else I can say. But I need you to find my babies."

"I got you. I promise."

Preach was circling in front of the door where Banks was resting inside after the surgery. To the moment no one but the doctors and Preach had entered the room for fear of contamination. But it didn't mean that various family members didn't hang around the door, wondering what was going on inside.

When the doctors finally exited Mason rushed up to them followed by Minnesota, Spacey, Derrick, Shay and Natty.

When they didn't speak right away Mason raised his arms in the air. "Well, what's going on now?"

"Uh, ummmmmm." Quincy said looking down.

The family stared at one another before focusing on the doctor.

Did Banks Wales die?

Preach stepped up. "Quincy, let me tell you something, drawing things out with us is the last thing you want. Now what's going on?"

One of the other doctors took a deep breath. "Let's just say as of this moment, it has gotten worse."

Mason leaned closer. "Excuse me, nigga?"

"I'll take it from here," Quincy said arrogantly. "First let me say we had no business doing this surgery. These are the types of things you do in a sterilized environment. Where he can be monitored."

"But you did though." Spacey said.

"True." Preach added.

"So, what are you telling us now?" Derrick asked Quincy.

"I'm saying we were forced, against our will, to do surgery in this house! And before doing it we explained the issues related to this type of procedure."

Mason's heart began to thump. "What does that fucking mean?"

"It means that things aren't working the way we hoped." Quincy said. "Since you want a straight up answer."

Thinking the worst, Mason and Preach pushed past them and entered the room to see for themselves. There on a hospital bed was Banks with his head bandaged and his face swollen two sizes too big.

Devastated, both Preach and Mason looked at one another while realizing they made a terrible mistake in greenlighting such a risky procedure. "Is this...this can't be Banks." Mason said mostly to himself. "He...he doesn't look like..."

"I know."

Slowly Preach and Mason walked out, closing the door behind them. "Why does he look like that?" Preach asked Quincy, while pointing at the door.

"You mean other than the reason that we just performed brain surgery? Literally."

"Oh, so you playing, nigga?" Derrick yelled.

"Let me tell you what's happening now." Mason said stepping up. "Your families are at an undisclosed location. If my friend dies, they'll die next."

"Please don't threaten us," one of the other doctors said. "We are already under pressure."

"We beyond that point." Preach said.

"Exactly," Mason continued. "If Banks doesn't make it, we will murder your families and bring you the pictures of their bodies. Only after you've cried every night for thirty days will we allow you out of your misery with a painful torturous death."

As Mason continued to talk to the doctors Minnesota took a deep breath. Pushing past the drama, she entered the room. She had to see her father for herself.

When she saw his swollen face, she dropped to her knees. Luckily Spacey and Shay were behind her and were able to help her to her feet.

"He's going to die." Minnesota whispered. "He's, he's actually going to die, and I will officially be all alone."

"I can't believe Mason and Preach allowed this to happen." Shay said holding her arms while rubbing them profusely. "Rev would never."

"Shut up," Minnesota said.

"I can't imagine life without him." Shay continued. "He can't die. He, he just can't die."

Natty who was also in the room rolled her eyes upon hearing her voice.

"Let's not make shit so final." Derrick said extending his palms to everyone. "The monitor is still beeping so that means his heart is pumping. And if his heart's still pumping, he's alive."

"But it looks like there's nothing else to be done." Shay said. "It, it looks like he's...he's fading away."

"We'll see about all that later." Spacey said loudly. "But for now, we need to remain strong. At the end of the day we don't need this kind of energy around him. And if he was up, he would tell us."

"I have to get out of here." Minnesota said turning for the door. "I have to get some air."

"We're coming with you." Derrick said.

When they walked past, Mason broke away from the doctors and said, "Wait, where are you going?"

"We just...I mean...we just need to get some air, pops." Derrick said. "Just for a little while." Natty, Shay, Minnesota and Spacey stood behind him.

"First of all, where's Joey?" Mason asked. He just realized he hadn't seen him.

"He heard about what happened and didn't wanna come." Spacey said. "I been keeping him updated on the phone though."

Mason sighed. "Well I think we should all stay here for now. So we can—"

"My father is in that room possibly dying. And unless you want me to go off...unless you want me to act out, I'm telling you I need some air." Minnesota said. "Please, just..."

"Let them go." Preach whispered putting a hand on Mason's shoulder.

Mason looked at him and back at the kids. His mind was so messed up about seeing Banks' face, that they both forgot about the war on the street. "Stay close."

By T. Styles

They nodded and walked out.

WALES ESTATE

Cassandra and Roxana jumped out of their cab and walked the grounds of the Wales land leading to the door. It was obvious that there had been no activity. Because back in the day you couldn't step foot on the property without being approached by a guard.

So where was everybody?

"Now do you believe me?" Roxana asked walking up to the door.

"What you talking about now?" Cassandra looked around carefully as they moved closer.

"When have you ever seen the property this empty? Something is up. They hiding."

"First off this is the second time we've come to their house." She whispered. "We don't know enough of what they do."

"Still."

They stopped walking. "Roxana, that doesn't mean anything is going on. You always look for conspiracy theories where there are none. I'll be glad when your medicine runs out because lately you talk too much."

"Just be quiet and come on."

Roxana approached the door and looked around. Slowly she turned the knob. It popped open and they walked   inside. This definitely shocked Cassandra. Because if she knew nothing else about the Wales', she knew that they prided themselves on their safety and security.

"Okay, you go right and look around and I'll go left." Roxana said. "That way we can cover more ground."

"Wait, what you talking about?" She whispered. "I think we should stay together."

"You act so scared."

"Roxana, you doing too much. Calm down."

"How? I mean, let's split up and see what we can find. And then we can meet back in the hallway."

"Roxana."

"Pleaseeeeee?" She said holding her hands together in a weird tight prayer mode. "I promise I won't be long."

By T. Styles

Cassandra wasn't feeling it one bit. "Listen, I don't want to have to come looking for you, Roxana. But I will if you make me. Meet me back here in five minutes tops. No more."

"Okay."

Roxana turned around and quickly headed down the corridors. She had only been in the home once, but paid attention to every detail. Within minutes, she found herself in Minnesota's room.

Amused, she placed her stuffed animal on the floor and traipsed towards her huge walk in closet. Immediately she was enamored by all of her designer purses, clothing and shoes.

Deeper and deeper into her closet she picked up and placed down different outfits. She always thought Minnesota was pretty but now seeing her style, since she had access to her room, she was enamored even more.

How she wished she had a similar lifestyle fitting of the rich and famous. In awe, she picked up a red dress and she removed her clothing quickly, opting to wear Minnesota's instead. After all, what was the use of being in a castle if she couldn't dress, feel and look like a queen?

Cassandra found herself in her brother's room. The moment she opened the door, without even looking in the closets she could tell he'd been there. It was his scent. It had an ocean like odor that wafted through the air like perfumed flowers.

Her brother had certainly been there, and she missed Tobias already.

But when she went to his closet, she was surprised to see hangers. In fact, there was only one pair of shoes toward the back. She knew they were his because they were the only pair of shoes he owned before moving to America. Sure, the pictures he sent showed the opulent lifestyle he was becoming accustomed to, but the shoes, well, the shoes were from home.

Her body trembled as she realized more and more that something happened to her brother. And that she may never see him again.

After more than the time allotted, Roxana came waltzing down the hall wearing Minnesota's dress. The moment Cassandra saw the change of clothing she went off in Spanish. "Wait, where are your clothes?"

"Gone." She twirled with a smile. "Do you like?"

"Gone?" She said through clenched teeth. "Are you fucking crazy?"

Roxana glared. "Don't say that to me."

"Well what you doing then? You were supposed to be searching for signs of Tobias."

"I know what I was supposed to be doing." She raised her arms and spun around again as if Cassandra didn't see her the first time. "But I found this and—"

"You're wearing her dress. That's gross. And it makes you look desperate. Don't you get it?"

Roxana rolled her eyes. "You are so boring."

She grabbed her forearm and squeezed. "I'm here to find Tobias. Not play around."

"Me too." She snatched away. "But...I mean...didn't you want to be like them just a little? Ever?"

"No. I'm quite happy being ourselves."

"I don't believe you."

"You don't have to believe me. This isn't our life. And it'll never be."

"I should've come by myself."

Cassandra felt badly that her sister wanted to be something other than who they were. "Roxana, I don't mean to be loud, but didn't you see how miserable they were on the island? Didn't you see the looks on their faces? With all the money they had they were still unhappy. Why would I want to trade that for anything? Especially possessions? Think."

Roxana looked down. "This life is different from ours."

"But does that make it better?"

"Back home, you can come and go as you please. But me...before the medicine, I was treated like the freak that nobody wants to be around."

"That's not true."

"You don't have to lie. I know it's true. And I guess, I guess I just wanted to wear the dress. Is that so hard to understand?"

She felt for her little sister. "You are so annoying."

"Tell me something I don't know already."

"No matter what, I want you to know I never looked at you like a freak. And I won't start now."

When they heard a soft noise, they decided to continue their search within the estate. Before long they ended up in front of a closed doorway. Did it lead up or down? Slowly Cassandra turned the knob and the moment she did they were yanked inside by two of Mason's men.

After toppling down, they landed in the basement.

"Who are you?" Billy asked as they maintained control of the sisters. "Huh? Who are you and what you doing here?"

"Get off of us!" Cassandra yelled.

"You're hurting my arm!" Roxana replied.

He squeezed Roxana a bit harder because she looked like a troublemaker. "I'm not gonna ask you again. Who are you?" He said more firmly.

"It doesn't matter who they are." Oliver, one of his other men said to Billy. "They're here because you were so busy trying to talk to the doctor's daughter that you left the door unlocked. This shit is not gonna end well I promise."

Billy released them. "If I were you, I wouldn't say that shit again." He pointed in his face.

"I just did."

"All I know is this, the last thing you want is Mason to be mad. Because if he finds out he won't just be fucked up with me. He'll be mad at you too."

He knew he was speaking gospel. "Okay, what you want me to do with them then?" He looked at Roxana and Cassandra. "Because one of us has to go back upstairs. Before somebody else comes in the house."

Billy thought for a minute. "Just take them in the room. They might as well get acquainted with the *others*. I'll find some rope down here to tie everybody up."

Roxana and Cassandra sat across from eight men and women who were trembling and crying as they held one another on the floor. Their backs were firmly against the wall.

"Who are you?" Cassandra asked in English. "And why do they have you here?"

By T. Styles

Silence.

"I think they're scared." Roxana whispered in Spanish.

Cassandra focused on the bunch. "We aren't here to hurt you." Cassandra persisted, scooting a little closer to the group, hoping that her voice could be shielded from their captors outside. "We're just here to find our brother. His name is Tobias."

Silence.

"They're getting on my nerves." Roxana said in Spanish. "Acting like punks."

"Shut up," Cassandra responded before focusing back on the crowd. "Maybe if you tell me why they have you held up; we can help each other. And get out of here together."

Silence.

"I don't think they know why they're here." Roxana whispered.

Cassandra took a deep breath. "I can't believe I let you bring me here." She said in her native language. "We never should've come. This is bad. Really bad."

The family members continued to look at them strangely. After all, they themselves weren't sure how they all connected. They only knew that they had doctors in their family. And because of this, they were called to help a very powerful man.

They also knew that if he died, they would die too.

Minnesota was driving Spacey's car as he sat in the passenger seat. In the back was Shay. Derrick was propped in the middle and Natty on the other end. Although Mason said they should stay near the house, before long they found themselves on the highway.

"How you doing?" Natty whispered to Derrick. "You look exhausted. Like you can barely keep your—"

"What difference does it make how he doing?" Shay asked leaning her head out to see past Derrick and directly at her. "It ain't his father who dying."

Natty frowned. "Last I remember, it ain't yours either."

"Oh, you snapping?" Shay was about to scratch her eyes out, but Derrick pushed her back into the window causing her to bump the back of her head.

"Cut all that dumb shit out!"

"Me?" Shay said pointing to herself.

"Listen, I'm just being friendly." Natty said to Shay with a sly smile. "It ain't about fighting or going against each other. We almost like family."

"First off, you not a part of *this* family." Shay said.

"And *you* are?"

Shay was annoyed. "If you ask me, you being a bit too friendly for my liking."

"Fuck I care about your liking? I ain't into women."

"Oh, so you admitting you are into Derrick!" Shay said loudly, as if she just won a high-profile case.

Nobody cared.

"Bitch, please."

"Let me make myself clear, NASSTTTYY NATTY. I don't know what you and Derrick had in the past, but that shit over."

"I'm really just here to be a support. I'm not trying to get in the way of anything ya'll got going on. Besides, I have my own drama."

"You say that but your whole face says trouble." She pointed at her. "And if I'm being honest, I don't like you very much." Shay continued.

"Like I said, you don't have to like me."

"Good because I don't."

"Can ya'll just stop for five minutes?" Minnesota asked. "Because contrary to what you both are saying, *my* father is dying and the last thing I need right now is any of this shit."

"I told you to let me drive." Spacey said looking over at his sister.

"I wanted to drive myself." She took a deep breath. "It's relaxing."

"That's because you like being in control." He looked out the window.

"Call it what you want. But I'm behind the wheel now."

Before they knew it, they were in front of the Wales estate. Minnesota parked and everyone piled out the car. Although they knew they probably shouldn't be home, the fellas wanted a drink from Banks' well-stocked bar and Minnesota wanted to grab a change of clothing instead of the weird outfit Mason gave her to wear after she killed Myrio.

Before they opened the front door, Minnesota said, "Maybe we should go around back."

"Why you say that?" Natty asked holding her hand between her legs, moving her feet rapidly. "I gotta pee."

"I don't know. But it doesn't hurt to be safe than sorry."

They walked around back instead.

CHAPTER ELEVEN
THE WALES ESTATE

Gary and Christopher sat in the back of the van on the way to Banks' crib. Christopher looked over at Gary and took a deep breath. He had been fidgety ever since they started the trip and it was making Gary annoyed.

"Are you sure about this, Gary?"

He shook his head and fell deeper into his seat. "Why would you ask me something like that?"

"I'm just saying, you never got over her. And for years you put me in a situation where I had to defend you. Is she worth this war?"

"I never asked you to defend me. You chose to be there, and I respected you for that decision."

"It doesn't take away from the point that I did defend you. And if I'm being honest it was really hard to watch you play yourself to get Nidia's attention."

"You know, unless you tell me differently, I'm starting to believe you're afraid. Everything about your body mechanics tells me so."

"You know I'm never afraid, Gary. You know that about me. I just hated how Nidia played you.

By T. Styles

The way you, well, always seemed to want to prove to her that you had her back."

"That was our business."

"It was still tough to watch, since we were cool before you met Nidia. I mean, she literally would have sex with you and then send you on your way. Like you were some cheap prostitute."

"I'm a grown man."

"I get that too. But I knew you were in love with her still. And now you're putting our lives on the line."

Finally, Gary believed he got to the heart of the matter. "I knew it. I was correct. You are afraid."

Christopher took a deep breath. "You call it what you want. I'm not going to try and change your mind."

"Nidia took care of us."

"I know that, Gary."

"Do you?"

"All I'm saying is—."

"You said enough!" Gary yelled, raising his hand and voice. "Now it's time to do some work."

Christopher remained silent as the cars parked in front of the Wales Estate. Luckily Minnesota and Billy's vehicle was in the garage.

When all of the soldiers piled out Gary looked at Christopher. "What you waiting on now?"

He frowned. "Did you need something?"

"Yes. I need for you to get out of the car."

Christopher leaned back because going into the house *first* was never the plan. "Wait, why? We have plenty of men."

"I want to make sure things go down correctly. And if it doesn't, I'm holding you responsible." He freed a cigarette from its pack and lit a square. "Now get the fuck out of the car."

Christopher took a deep breath. There was no use in fighting him. Besides, they had traveled all the way from Texas for this day. So, he reluctantly pushed the door open and then entered the house with the rest of the men.

As they were gone, sitting in the truck alone, Gary thought about what Christopher said. He hated hearing the truth. He *was* in love with Nidia from the moment he laid eyes on her pretty face. And yet, she always seemed to have this weird obsession with Banks Wales.

An obsession she couldn't escape.

Before her demise, each week would pass, and he would try his best to prove that he was worth her time. But she never cared. Nidia wanted one

174

man and one man only even though he was unavailable.

After reminiscing for what seemed like forever Gary was annoyed.

Where was everyone? He thought.

And so, he decided to go see for himself.

Bolero stood at the door of the Wales estate with his men, preparing to enter as if they were the swat team. When he nodded, all of his men rushed inside the premises.

It was time for war.

"Cars are out front so look everywhere for them!" Bolero said firmly, entering the estate as if it were his own. "And bring everybody to my feet. Alive. Or dead. It doesn't matter."

Although he was moving swiftly on getting revenge, without talking to Banks to verify Tobias' whereabouts, he felt justified.

Upon Bolero's word, the men nodded and went throughout the house to fulfill his request. But a minute later, Gary and Christopher, followed by their men, appeared in front of him. They were covered in splattered blood.

Gary's men aimed at Bolero, ready to cut him down.

"Who are you?" Gary questioned.

Bolero was stunned at the stranger and his firepower. Had he not moved irresponsibly, he would've told some of his men to remain and now he was alone. "The question I should be asking is who the hell are you?"

"As far as I can see I have more firepower." Gary said arrogantly. "So, do you really want to go there?"

The moment he said that Bolero's men returned aimed and ready. They rushed to the scene with their weapons. It definitely looked like a war was about to ensue.

"Listen, we have business here," Bolero said. "And unless you are with Banks, which I'm assuming you're not, I have no problem with you as of now. Please don't make that change."

Gary looked at the weaponry and said, "Well, judging by the firepower I don't believe that's true."

"One could say the same about you." Bolero said calmly looking at his men and their guns. "But like I said I'm here for the Wales family. Where are they?"

"Hold up, I have a few questions." Gary said loudly. "Like what issues do you have with them?"

"That's none of your business. The only thing you need be concerned about is what's going to happen next."

Gary and Bolero stared at each other for what seemed like forever. Finally believing he could take them, in Spanish Bolero instructed his men to kill.

Hercules was driving up on the property until he heard the gun battle inside the Wales Estate. Quickly he about faced in his Benz and got away from the scene as soon as possible. He didn't know what was happening inside, but he definitely knew based on the sound that he was outmanned and outgunned.

It was time to bounce.

About two miles away from the property he called Gina. "Mother, something has gone on at the estate."

"What does that mean exactly?"

"I don't know the details. All I know for sure is I was about to look for them like you asked and I decided to slide by the house first."

"Slide by the house? But what if you were seen or followed?"

"I would've been fine."

"Go ahead…" She was angry and he knew it.

"Anyway, when I got there, I heard a gun battle. I'm not sure if anybody inside is alive."

Silence.

"Mother."

"Are you sure it was gunfire?"

"We spent our childhood at the range. It was gun fire. If I had to be exact, I would say a few nines, forty fives and some—"

"Don't be smart, Hercules."

"It's not about being smart. It's about using past experience to judge a situation. And I'm telling you I heard fire. You can believe me, or you can come here to check for yourself."

Silence.

"Mother, what now?"

"Were there cars outside the home?"

"Many."

"How many would you say?"

By T. Styles

"More than what's necessary."

"Banks is in trouble."

He took a deep breath. "Could be."

"Come home right away."

"I'm already in route."

THE PETIT ESTATE
1972

It was a beautiful day when Angie decided that she no longer felt like being sad. She played the sock game a few times, but even that provided her reduced joy. So, when she heard a machine running, she grew excited, figuring it was her crush.

Crawling toward the window, she remained on her knees as she looked out. If someone was staring from the outside, only her eyes would be seen.

There on the lawn of Mrs. Fischer's property was Peteery. He was trimming the bushes and singing gleefully as he worked. There was a large yellow plastic cup near, which he sipped from every now and again.

It was moonshine.

When he paused to wipe the sweat off his brow, she stood on her feet. And for some reason, he looked up and saw her vanilla colored body in the window. It resembled a Salvador Dali painting, except the view was from the front not the back.

Realizing she caught his attention, unlike in the past, she felt inspired enough to remove her cotton pajama top. Her body seemed to glow from the inside and her brown nipples erected as they brushed against the pane.

Amazed at what he was witnessing, Peteery dropped the hedge trimmer and continued to watch from a far. When he sensed she was about to go away, he nodded up and down eagerly begging for more.

In the mood to please, she removed her pajama bottoms, exposing the brown hairy crest between her legs.

Wanting to play a special game, it was now she who nodded once.

He removed his shirt. His muscles were complete.

She nodded again.

By T. Styles

He looked around, dropped his pants a little and removed his long, thick penis. She pressed against the frame, begging with her eyes to see more.

He nodded.

She smiled.

Reenacting what she saw on the magazine, she rubbed her breast and pinched her nipple, causing it to push through her fingertips like a jackfruit's stem.

Before long she noticed the more she caressed her breasts, the more he stroked his dick and that it was lengthened with each pull. Just the act of pleasuring him from a far, caused her body to heat up in ways she didn't know was possible.

As the moment continued, the pane fogged up with her passionate breath as she experienced heightened sensations. The sock didn't stand a chance. This was so much more exciting. With her free hand, she stroked her hairy mound, tiptoeing over her clit with each move until it was so tender it was almost too sensitive to touch.

Quicker and faster she went until suddenly she witnessed him cascade over his fingertips just as she orgasmed too. From his dick came a long stream of cream that immediately brought him to his knees.

Ashamed, he pulled up his pants and ran away.

While she slid to the floor, out of breath, with a smile on her face.

After fighting with her husband about Angela's confinement, she was forced to let her out for dinner. Although she was against releasing her from isolation, she was certain she would mess up again and that she would be well within her right to throw her back where she belonged.

And so, Angela, Gina, Hercules and Morgan sat at the dinner table preparing to eat a meal. Angela thumbed through fish that smelled so dank it was tough to think about eating, let alone placing in her mouth.

"Eat, Angie," Gina said.

Silence.

Morgan cleared his throat. "How are you, sweetheart?" He tore into his roll which once again was the only edible food on the table.

Hercules looked at his sister, waiting for an answer.

"I'm fine, daddy."

By T. Styles

Gina smirked hoping to set her off, to show how unstable she was. "What exactly does fine mean?" She wiped her mouth with her linen napkin and took a large gulp of red wine.

"What do you want it to mean, mother?" She asked with a lowered gaze.

"Well, it's not what I want, it is what you feel."

"Leave it alone, dear." Morgan said.

"Why should I?"

"Maybe because I want to keep the peace."

"Morgan, she smells like trash." She looked at Angela. "I mean, why wouldn't you bother to wash up for dinner? Like I asked?"

Angela laughed under her breath.

Gina looked at Morgan. "Do you see now? She isn't well."

"Oh, Gina, please."

"Please what? This is ripping us a—."

Suddenly Angela pushed her plate to the floor, and it shattered into a million pieces. With a resounding thud, she slammed her left foot on the table, followed by the right. The soles of her feet were so black it looked like she was wearing shoes.

"Angie!" Gina yelled standing up.

"What, mother?" She said slyly.

"Get your feet off of the table this instance!"

WAR 7: PINK COTTON 183

Instead of obeying, she raised her skirt and exposed her mound. Since she wasn't wearing panties, her vagina showed as clear as the entrees in the center. Taking her fingertips over her button she said, "I guess I'm sexual after all huh, mother?"

Morgan quickly stood up and grabbed Hercules, rushing him away from the scene. But he looked back once, needing to keep the view to memory.

When they were gone Gina walked up to her and slapped her in the face. "It will be a long time before I allow you back with my family."

"Mother, I could care less." She had Peteery. Who cared about isolation?

In the moment Gina wished she never had her as a daughter. She proved how much she hated her, when she kept her in the room for a week with no food and little water.

On the seventh day she finally entered the garret.

Angela was sitting on the floor starving. She lost so much weight she could barely hold her head up due to fatigue. "Mother, please..."

"Please what?"

"I'm sorry."

"What are you sorry for?"

"Being nasty."

By T. Styles

Gina glared. "Never cross me again. Because if you do, I will destroy you. And no one will ever find your flesh because I will bury you within the walls."

She tossed her an orange and walked away.

CHAPTER TWELVE
BIRTHING CENTER

Mason stood next to Jersey's bedside. She was going into labor and having contractions pretty far apart. Originally, he had no intentions of being there for her but with Banks' condition being up in the air he wanted to be there for his friend by being there for his *wifey*.

"You know you don't have to do this right?" Jersey asked as she rubbed her belly. She was certain her little girl would be born within a few hours. "I know things are crazy now and—."

"I know I don't have to be here." Mason took a seat in the recliner and ran his hand down his face. "And you know I don't do anything I don't want to. I'm, I guess, I'm doing this for Banks. Besides, the baby is coming early."

"The doctor says she's fine. Will just have to stay here longer." She shook her head. "What did you mean by doing *this* for Banks? It sounds so, so bizarre."

He shrugged. "Nothing about our lives are normal that's for sure."

By T. Styles

"I can't believe it but for some reason it seems like we're closer now than we were as a married couple." She looked at him. "Why is that? Why are we better as, whatever this is?"

He took a deep breath. "To tell you the truth I don't know why. You can't question everything."

"I'm not trying to nag."

"I know...I know. I also realize you like answers." He sighed deeply. "If I had to pick a reason it would probably be because, I think, I mean, all of us relied too much on Banks."

"I don't understand."

"Speaking for myself, it was all I cared about. It's all I care about now."

She nodded finally hearing the truth he denied throughout their relationship. "I get it."

"And now we have to deal with the possibility of...not being able to rely on him." He resituated himself. "Because even if he makes it back..."

"With brain surgery there's nothing to say he'll be the same." She said finishing his thoughts.

It hurt.

"Exactly." He sighed deeply. "Other than that, with me and you having problems in the past, I guess in some ways I resented you for not being the woman I thought you should be. The woman I needed. I was able to control you, Jersey. To have my way all the time. And I needed something else."

She looked down and rubbed her belly. "Now you tell me."

"It's not that I'm telling you now and not then." He sat up. "It's just that you're either that type of person who stands her ground or not. And you weren't. You can't fake that kind of thing, you understand?"

"Wow." She felt stupid for allowing him to take advantage for so long.

"I'm not trying to hurt your feelings."

"No, I get it." She nodded. "And I resented you for forcing me to be weaker than I felt inside. I don't know..." she shrugged. "I guess, I wanted to move in life with the least bit of confrontation. And I'm finally realizing that anything great is worth being uncomfortable for."

"What you mean?"

"If everything is easy where is the joy when you finally get what you desire?" She sighed. "I didn't think this would be our story but I'm happy that at least we can—."

Mason's phone rang. "Hold up, Jersey." He looked at the screen, hoping to see Preach's number and it would be good news. It wasn't him. "What's up, Scoop? I'm kinda busy right—."

"Something is going on at the Wales Estate."

He frowned and stood up. "What you talking about? We got people sitting on the house because—"

"It looks like it's on fire, sir."

He looked at Jersey and then focused back on the call. "That's impossible," he whispered. He walked further away from her bedside. Although she was still looking his way eager to find out what was happening. "Like I said, we have men there looking over things." He thought about the doctors' families that he held up there until he was sure Banks was good. And at the same time, he told Preach that Billy and Oliver were more than likely not the men for the job.

He was learning that he may be correct.

"I'm telling you the house is on fire. Literally. And from what I'm being told Minnesota and...I mean..."

"Just say it, nigga!"

"Minnesota, Derrick and Spacey may be inside."

"How you know that?" He yelled.

"I talk to Minnesota's friend Natty from time to time. And she hit me up earlier saying they were on the way."

Mason felt like he had dropped fifty feet.

He forgot to warn the kids about Bolero.

It was a big mistake.

Not wanting to alarm Jersey more than he already had he took the phone from his ear and walked toward her. "Listen. I have to take this call right quick." He pointed at it.

"Okay."

"But I'll be back later to check on you."

She rubbed her stomach. "Well, is everything, I mean..."

"I gotta go."

"What's going on, Mason? More bad news?"

"Like I said, I have to take care of some things." He was a bit firmer, to let her know this was not up for discussion. "That's all I can say right now."

"Should I be worried? Because if you leave the way you are, I'm going to, Mason. Please don't let anything happen to my son."

"Trust me. I got us."

Mason didn't want to believe more danger was hitting his family and so he was speeding quickly on the way to the Wales Estate. He knew that if the news was true, that the estate was on fire, then that meant they lost their leverage with the doctors.

And what about Derrick, Minnesota and Spacey?

Were they safe?

When the phone rang, he quickly answered but regretted it directly afterwards when he heard the caller's voice. "Mason, where have you been? I have been worried sick. This is so unfair to me."

He sighed deeply. "Now is not the time, Dasher."

"It's never the right time with you is it?"

"Not now." He repeated more firmly.

"I'm serious! But guess what, that's not going to be good enough. I'm on my way to your house as we speak."

He was so angry he saw black. "Please don't go to my place. Things are not good right now."

"I'm more confused than ever."

"I'm not gonna be able to see you for a while. You hear me? It just ain't happening."

"I just said I'm—,"

"I know what you said. But you better not show up."

"Are you threatening me?"

"If I threaten you, you'll feel me."

"Good, because I already told you we aren't doing the breakup shit anymore."

He made a left and merged onto the highway. "I'm not talking about breaking up. But I am talking about putting some space between us. Like I said, my life is hectic. But the moment things clear up I'll explain."

"Okay, well now you make me feel a little better. When are you going to let me be there for you?"

"You can be there for me now by listening to what I'm telling you." He hung up.

Mason hit the gas and drove faster.

His heart rate kicked up when he saw each passing sign.

As he rushed to the scene, now he realized what Banks had to go through worrying about so many people. Not having him there as a spine put many things into perspective. He finally saw what it meant to wear the crown.

To *really* wear the crown.

He finally saw what it meant to be king. And he was no longer interested in the power.

All he wanted was things to be as they used to be, before his man fell ill.

When a new call came through, he quickly answered without looking. "Who is it?"

"Dad, it's me. Derrick!" His voice was hysterical, and Mason had to pull over to prevent crashing.

"Where are you? At the Wales?"

"I was at first. There was so much going on at the house! Bolero and his men came into Banks' crib along with some other dudes we believe were with Nidia. They got to busting off and...I don't know...it was crazy!"

"Are you safe?"

"Yes! But we don't get what's going on! We on our way to the house now. To hide out for a little while!"

"No! Don't go to our crib."

"Why?"

"Don't ask why. Go back to Jersey's estate. Where I can look after you."

"Dad, my clothes are a mess. We had to run through dirt and shit and I just wanna freshen up so—."

"I said no, Derrick. Do what the fuck I'm telling you. Now who's with you?"

He took a deep breath. "Uh, Minnesota, Spacey, Shay and Natty. Everybody shaken up."

Mason was relieved. "That's good. Stay together and do exactly as I say. Don't make no more stops."

Sitting in the passenger seat, Bolero was following Derrick from behind. One of his men, the only one who escaped alive along with him, was driving.

Bolero was not in a good place mentally.

After the gun battle Bolero and his only surviving employee rushed through the house. When he saw some strangers and Roxana and Cassandra lying in a pile, he lost his mind.

He wanted it burned to the ground.

And so, he did.

By T. Styles

After setting the Wales Estate on fire, he thought he would need to take time to consider a new brand of revenge until he saw the Wales and Louisville children drive away from the scene.

He immediately traced them from afar. "Don't follow so closely but don't lose them either," Bolero said in Spanish.

The driver fell back a little. "Sorry, boss. I just didn't want to lose them."

"I get that, but we don't want them to see us either."

He nodded and took a deep breath. He was still greatly shaken up by the scene at the house. "I understand."

"When they finally know we're tailing them, I want it to be too late."

CHAPTER THIRTEEN

Shay was crying softly in the backseat as Derrick piloted the car. As she heard her weeping, Minnesota grew annoyed. Not because she didn't understand the gravity of what was happening. But because she was finally realizing crying was a waste of energy. Especially if crying was a normal thing, as it had been with Shay. She was being so weird she wondered if she was pregnant.

"I can't believe this shit happening." Derrick said as he consistently looked out of the rearview mirror. He saw many cars trailing him but peeped nothing suspicious. "We almost got dusted. I wonder who the fuck that was? And who did they kill in the house?"

"It's got to be Bolero's men," Minnesota said. "They probably looking for Tobias."

"But who were they fighting?" Derrick persisted.

"Whoever it was, shit was way too real for us." Spacey continued. "Had we not heard them talking, we would be an afterthought."

Silence filled the car for a moment as they considered the grave thought.

"So, what will happen next?" Natty asked. "Because although I like you all, I don't want to die because of you."

"Then you shouldn't have gotten in the car." Shay said, sniffling. "Because for real, for real, I don't remember anybody asking you to jump in." She leaned her head against the window. "I wish they took your ass out."

"Jumping in the car and hearing your mouth is the price I paid." Natty wanted to say more but decided to say less.

"Do you think they will go after Dad?" Shay asked Spacey. "Because for them to come in the house, they had to be after him, right?"

"Why you think that?" Derrick asked.

"I just told you. It was Dad's house!"

Minnesota didn't want to let on that she saw Banks kill Tobias. Not yet anyway. "Let's not make up a bunch of hypotheticals."

"Yeah, they gotta find him first which ain't happening." Spacey said. "But we definitely gotta be on guard. For him and us."

"Fuck!" Derrick yelled hitting the steering wheel.

"What's wrong with you now, boy?" Shay asked.

"Why don't you have any gas?" Derrick questioned Minnesota with an attitude.

"First of all, I didn't think we would be driving my car. But since somebody shot up Spacey's we had to take it."

"You aren't answering the question. Why the fuck don't you have gas? I hate that shit about females." He looked at his girlfriend. "Always driving on E."

"There you go putting me in shit again." Shay said.

"Listen, this my sister's car, man." Spacey said. "Period. If she doesn't have gas, she doesn't have gas."

"Well I'm pulling over at a station. Otherwise we gonna be stranded."

"Do whatever you have to do." Spacey responded just wanting him to shut the fuck up. "But make it quick." He looked out of his window. "I got a bad feeling."

When they made it to the gas station, they all piled out. Natty walked into the store to get some cigarettes with Spacey and Derrick. While Shay strolled up to Minnesota. "I don't like your friend."

Minnesota rolled her eyes. "I get all that."

"I'm serious. I wish you never brought her back into the picture."

"Shay, please cut out all the complaining. Okay?" She took a deep breath. "I'm worried about my father. All this other shit is not on my list."

"I'm worried about dad too."

"Well prove it by leaving me alone." She paused. "Now I gotta make a call right quick."

"Who you hitting up?"

She removed her cell from her pocket. "Somebody important." Minnesota walked a few feet away. Shay remained close although she couldn't hear who she was calling.

When Minnesota was done, she was about to head back to the car when she spotted Bolero inside a vehicle in front of the station.

Her heart dropped.

Instead of going back to her ride she yelled, "RUUUUUUNNNNNNNN!"

When Bolero's soldier saw them, he fired. But she and Shay immediately took off in the opposite direction. The two young women were fast and motivated to stay alive making them an impossible target to hit.

The other members of their crew, Spacey and Derrick weren't so lucky. Bolero's hitman was able to catch them inside the store, and as a result he fired five rounds into their direction.

A few of his bullets landed.

Minnesota and Shay were sitting in a stranger's backyard, on lawn chairs, waiting for Natty. After the shootout they were able to break ground but lost their family. Two hours later, Natty hit her and said she was able to get her car from the hotel and would be on her way. But Minnesota's nerves were bad.

While pulling up a few grass blades Shay said, "I'm so scared, Minnie."

She looked at her sternly. "What I tell you about calling me that shit?"

She shrugged. "I'm sorry. It's a habit."

"That doesn't have nothing to do with me. Call me by my full name or don't call me at all." Minnesota continued to look for her friend's car but didn't see her anywhere in sight.

She tucked her hair behind her ear. "What is it about the nickname that you don't like?"

By T. Styles

"A lot."

"Give me a few things."

She didn't feel like talking and at the same time, if she was talking it meant Shay wasn't. "For starters, people call me Minnie to keep me in line. But I'm a grown woman. So, it won't work no more."

When Natty finally pulled up Minnesota sighed in relief as they ran in the direction of her silver Benz.

Once at the curb, Minnesota quickly eased into the front passenger seat. She hugged her friend and breathed another sigh of relief. "How you get away?"

"Girl, I ran out the backdoor of the gas station."

"Is my brother okay? And Derrick?"

"Like I said when I first hit you, I don't know. I caught an Uber, grabbed my car and came back to get you. You still haven't talked to them yet?"

She looked down. "No, he hasn't answered the phone. And now I'm starting to get worried."

When Shay tried to ease into the car by pulling on the door handle, Natty locked it quickly. "Stupid bitch, I'm sick of her ass," she said to Minnesota.

Her eyes widened. "What you doing? Let her in! We have to get out of here!"

"I know." She pouted.

"So, open the fucking door!"

"That bitch has gotten on my nerves all day." She stabbed a fist into her palm. "I'm not letting her in my car until she apologizes."

Minnesota threw her weight back in her seat.

Shay, on the other hand, was clueless about the controversy brewing inside and took to pulling on the door handle repeatedly like a madman wondering why she couldn't enter.

She didn't stop yanking until Natty rolled the window down halfway. "You owe me an apology or you not getting in."

Shay frowned. "What?"

"So, you wanna play stupid? You wanna act like all the shit you been doing ain't been smart out the face?"

"I have no idea what you talking about." Shay said, crossing her arms tightly over her chest.

"Put it this way, I'm not letting you get into my car unless you apologize for how you've been treating me all day. Or you can eat a dick and die slow."

"I can't believe this." Minnesota said from the inside. "We got people hunting us and you doing this now?"

By T. Styles

Natty looked at her. "Look, I fuck with you, Minnesota."

"I know you do."

"Good, but I could never stand that girl and you know that too. And as much as you care about her, for whatever reason, I would rather reach in my pocket and give her cash to catch a cab before I allow her to sit in my car. Now I'm willing to change my mind but she has to apologize."

"She my sister, Natty."

"I'm your sister." She said putting her hand over her heart. "After all the things we been through together, *I'm* your sister. I took a bullet for you and we still cool. But I don't fuck with that bitch."

Natty focused on the open window. "Are you gonna apologize or not? We don't have all day."

"What is wrong with you?" Shay said throwing her hands up. "This is a weird ass flex if you ask me."

"I'm still waiting."

"I ain't with the shits."

"Just apologize, Shay!" Minnesota yelled across Natty.

"I'm not gonna apologize for wanting this bitch to stay away from me and my man."

"I don't want your man." Natty said.

"Sure, you don't, wet tissue."

Natty glared. "Well, I guess we'll see you at the house." She put the car in drive. "Let's get out of—."

"Wait!" Shay yelled.

Natty parked. "I'm waiting."

"I apologize or whatever." She said under her breath.

"That's not going to be good enough, sweet fart."

Shay rolled her eyes. And as if it were the hardest thing, she ever had to do in the world she said, "I apologize."

"For what?" Natty continued.

"For getting on your nerves all day."

"Good, the girl apologized." Minnesota said. "Now let her in so we can leave."

Having gotten her way, Natty smiled and unlocked the door. And Shay, super irritated jumped inside and slammed the door so hard her window rattled.

Natty rotated quickly in her direction. "Bitch, don't make me put you out again!"

"I'm sorry." She said crossing her arms again.

"Can we please get to the house?!"

CHAPTER FOURTEEN
JERSEY'S ESTATE

Preach paced the floor as he was talking to Mason on the phone. He couldn't believe the amount of drama that kicked off since he been held up at Jersey's estate while they were waiting on word of Banks' condition.

The last he heard, Minnesota, Spacey, Derrick, Shay and Natty were going for a quick drive. Some hours later, the Wales Estate burned down, the police were hitting Banks' phone about the fire and Mason was shook.

"I don't get this shit," Mason said. "Nobody was outside when Banks did Tobias but us, Minnesota and Myrio. That lil nigga gone so how did Bolero find out?"

Preach took a deep breath and coughed. "I don't know. I feel like we covered our tracks. I guess we dropped the ball somehow."

"This bad."

"You telling me." Preach paused and looked at the door where the doctors were inside with Banks. "Since they family gone, what you want me to do about the doctors?"

By T. Styles

"I'm gonna leave that to your judgement. I trust you."

Preach nodded. "Okay. What you about to do now?"

"I have to find out what's up with my son. He not there yet?"

"Nah."

"I got a bad feeling." He paused. "Just make a decision on the doctors ASAP."

When Preach got off the phone he continued to pace the floor outside Banks' door. When it finally opened, and the doctors walked out, he took a deep breath.

"Okay, ya'll mothafuckas been in there all day. Now what's happening? Because I'm sick of waiting."

Quincy stepped up arrogantly as usual. "He's not meeting the standard that makes us believe that he will survive."

Preach felt gut-punched. It was obvious at this point that Banks Wales was going to die. And it was also obvious that he was too much of a punk to tell him straight up.

"Okay, I understand. Well, I guess you did all you can for now. I'll allow you to be with your families."

WAR 7: PINK COTTON

The doctors smiled.

When they walked through the house and into the kitchen, they stood in the middle of the floor. Preach was in front of them. Within seconds, Preach's men walked behind the doctors.

"What's this about?" Quincy laughed once.

"What you mean? I want you to be with your families." Preach nodded at the men. "Ain't that what you want?"

"So, you're letting us leave?" One of the doctors asked. "Like out of here? Because, because this feels off."

"In a sense." Preach nodded again.

"Okay, you're making me nervous now." Quincy said.

"I don't want you to be nervous." Preach responded. "I don't want you to be anything actually. At the end of the day you failed, and we told you what failing would mean."

"Okay, but he isn't gone yet," Quincy smiled, trying to talk his way out. "Let us see if we can do anything more."

"So, you saying my friend is awake?"

"No, I said he's in a bad way but he's still alive. Give us some time to make sure he'll—"

Before he could finish his sentence one by one the doctors were killed with a bullet to the back of the head. A half an hour later, the earth behind Jersey's house that was dug up earlier, was filled with their severed body parts.

When he saw they were covered, he slowly walked back into the house. First, he checked on his father who was asleep and looking as if he were having some trouble breathing.

Next he checked on Banks.

Standing in front of the door he finally walked into the room. Sitting in a chair next to his bed, he listened to the weak heart monitor beeping slowly.

He could tell it was just a matter of time.

"I never got a chance to tell you what you meant to me." Preach nodded. "And...and I'm not gonna do that now. I just want you to know that as long as I'm alive your children will be taken care of. I'll see to it. I'll lay my life down on the line for them, Banks." He positioned himself to turn off the machines. "Rest easy my—"

When there was a knock at the door Preach's men ran to the room. "Do you want me to answer it?" One of them asked.

He dropped his hand that was hovering the button of the breathing machine "Did you see who it was?"

"No, we came straight to you first."

He removed his weapon from his waist. "Be ready to cover me."

"For sure."

Slowly they walked toward the entrance. Once there, who he saw shocked them all. It was Gina Petit, and she was flanked with cops.

Opening the door because he knew there was no use in running, he frowned. He looked into her eyes, and then the eyes of the six officers she brought with her. "What you doing here, Gina? Or is that even your real name?"

She laughed.

"I asked what you doing here?" Preach said firmer. "And where are the twins?"

"They are where they are. And you know why I'm here. Now where is Banks? I need to save his life."

He frowned. "How did you, well how did you know?" He coughed.

She took a deep breath. "My great-granddaughter called."

He leaned in closer. "Minnesota hit you?"

By T. Styles

"I was as shocked as you are, but after hearing what's going on, I'm glad she did. You know, I've been looking for him since yesterday. And I never thought about coming here." She sighed. "Now, where is he?"

Preach frowned as he thought about what Minnesota had done.

"Don't be angry with Minnesota." Gina said. "She did what's for the best. Because, well, let's just say I can help forcefully, or this can be easy." She looked back at the officers and then Preach. "I know you care about your friend. Take the second option."

Preach didn't know if he should be mad or relieved. Because after seeing Banks' condition, he was done.

"What are you planning to do?"

"So, let me tell you how this is going to go down. I'm taking Banks, who I have been told is in this house dying. And you are going to let him go and you are going to tell Mason he died."

"What?"

"I'm not done." Gina said raising her head. "And when I do this, you will let him go. Forever."

"And if I don't?"

"I'll walk away. And the man you say you care about, will perish. Is that what you really want?"

Preach coughed again. "If he dies, I will find you."

"That's fair and I believe you."

"I don't care if you believe me or not."

She glared and raised her chin. "What are you going to do?"

"I'm gonna allow him to go. But no matter what happens, he will always remember us. We are his real family."

"May I come in? Or will we run over you?"

Now this was the power money possessed. Because within thirty minutes of leaving Jersey's estate, Gina had Banks surrounded by the best doctors' inside of an urgent care facility which they closed down. Although things looked bleak, they assured her they would try their best, but he was in for a tough ride.

Besides, there were many things happening in the moment. For starters there was too much fluid

212   *By T. Styles*

on Banks' brain and as a result, he had a ten percent chance of survival.

But she didn't care.

She wanted to try.

After they did all they could to relieve the pressure on his brain, Banks was taken to the Petit Estate. In a large room surrounded by nurses and 24-hour care, he had stabilized but it didn't mean that if he were to survive that he wouldn't be a vegetable.

"I can't believe all of this is happening." Hercules said walking up to Banks' bedside. Gina was on the opposite end.

"What are you running your mouth about now, Hercules?" Gina said touching Banks' hand.

"This is way out there." He clasped his hands behind his back. "Even for you."

"Why you say that?"

"You have turned our home into a hospital unit for one. Not to mention the ramifications, Mother. This is a powerful man. And powerful men are valuable. Someone will come looking for him."

"First off, I'm not worried about the ramifications. Because if something happened to you, I would do the same."

"How do you know people won't find out he's here? For instance, what about Minnesota?"

"I've instructed her that if she wants my help, she must remain silent."

"And you believe she will?"

"I do. Although she may need a little help."

"I still think you're going too far."

"Remind me about that when someone tries to perform brain surgery on you."

"This is a dangerous game you're playing with him."

"I have plans. Plans that exceed anything Banks can envision. I mean look at him. He's perfect."

Hercules looked at Banks and had to admit he was very attractive. And at the same time, he couldn't get over the days he followed him before letting Gina know that he knew they were related.

During those days Banks was all male and he would never see him as anything different. "Okay, I'll play along. What now?"

"Well, for starters I'm going to nurse him back to health." She sighed. "Now, have you found your sister?"

He drank most of the water and sat the cup on the table. Wiping his mouth with the back of his hand he said, "No."

"I'm getting more concerned." She sighed deeply. "Honestly, she's been known to do this type of thing before, but never this long. At the very least she would've returned for money. And I'm starting to think that maybe she's being held against her will."

"You don't think Banks and them are involved do you?"

"No. I don't. And at the same time when Minnesota called, she seemed to be aware of who I was, even if she didn't know about my wealth. So, I know they were onto me, but I don't think it was until after I left." She touched Banks' hand. "I'm gonna hold onto hope that this is one of her ways of trying to get more money out of me. Because you and I both know she's done that before."

"Bringing this man here seems bad for our family. I hope I'm wrong."

THE PETIT ESTATE

Per Gina's request, an hour later Spacey and Minnesota were inside the Petit residence for a secret meeting. Spacey was apprehensive at first and wore a stern look on his face as he entered.

But after learning that Derrick was shot and Spacey was almost hit, Minnesota wanted her brother at her side to be sure he was safe. Besides, it was Gina's idea. Only after swearing him to secrecy about not telling anyone that Banks was alive did she agree to take him.

But Spacey was beefing with Gina. After all, he hated being duped. By an old lady at that. He couldn't help but recall all of the conversations they had where she coerced him into getting married. He felt stupid remembering the mental games she played.

He didn't trust the woman one bit and yet standing at his father's bedside, looking at his face, he couldn't help but feel relief that at the very least the swelling had gone down.

By T. Styles

He looked, dare he'd say, normal.

Perhaps Gina wasn't so bad after all. They were standing in the room Banks was in when Gina said, "She looks good doesn't she?"

"Why do you keep saying that?" Minnesota frowned. "*He* looks good. And the answer is yes."

"Sorry. I mix up my words from time to time." Gina said before coughing. "I guess I'm still hung up on him being born a woman."

Spacey gazed at Minnesota.

"Who told you who I was?" Gina asked.

"Preach told me. When I was looking for my brother."

"So, your entire time with us was a lie?" Spacey asked quietly as to not disturb his father even though he was in a coma.

"I understand why you're upset." Gina said.

"You have no idea why we're upset." Minnesota responded. "We trusted you. And thought you were a friend."

"You thought I was a nanny."

"But you still lied." Spacey said firmly.

"True." Gina nodded. "And still, Minnesota trusted me enough to call and save your mother's life."

"This is my father." Minnesota said. "Not my mother."

"Again, I get confused."

Silence.

"This is crazy." Spacey said shaking his head. "Like I really can't believe you're our great-grandmother."

"Why? Because I'm white?"

"Kinda." Minnesota shrugged. "I mean I knew dad was biracial, but we never really met that part of our family."

"That makes me sad. It really does. But let me tell you everything you need to know. About me. About your great-grandfather. About your heritage as a Petit." She said raising her chin.

"We not feeling none of this." Minnesota said.

"You're hurt now. I can see it in your eyes. But I'm sure with time everything will come into understanding, with my help."

"We have to go." Spacey said.

"Stay a bit longer. And look after your mot...I mean father."

"What about my friend?" Minnesota said. "She's outside waiting to take us back."

"No, she isn't. I sent her away."

JERSEY'S ESTATE

Mason rushed in the house after getting an urgent call from Preach. He had been with his son getting stitched up by their on-call doctor. In the shootout, Derrick took a few bullets to the arm but was alive.

The moment Mason saw his face he knew the worst had been realized.

That his friend, Banks Wales, was gone.

"I'm sorry, man." Preach said walking up to him slowly. "I'm...I'm sorry."

"No...no...you can't play with me."

He ran into the room that held his body.

His legs felt like cooked spaghetti trying to hold up his frame when he saw Banks was gone. Holding the sides of his face he felt dizzy.

Derrick, Shay, and Joey walked into the room followed by Preach.

Mason turned to him. "Please, please don't tell me that...that he's..."

"I'm sorry, man," Preach said.

"Please don't tell me that my man is gone."

Joey frowned. "What...I'm...what's happening? Where is my father? I thought...I thought...Spacey said the surgery...I..."

Mason rushed up to Preach and grabbed his shirt. "Please, man. I don't understand."

"They said they tried all they could do but, in the end...in the end he didn't make it."

There was an uproar.

A painful wailing cry by everyone present. Even Derrick shed a tear before grabbing Shay to prevent her from hitting the ground. Which caused the stitches from his gunshot wound in his arm to rip suddenly.

The sound was horrible.

And afterwards, for whatever reason, no one said an audible word, having to stew into a new way of life. A lifestyle that no one was equipped to handle.

A life without Banks Wales.

Suddenly Joey walked away from the group and threw up in the corner of the room. Afterwards, he simply left the estate.

More silence filled the room and then Mason looked at Preach's face. Something in his disposition made him believe he was lying.

By T. Styles

Going off gut, he quickly removed his gun and rushed him knocking him to the floor with a slam to the face. Cocking his weapon, he asked, "Where the body at, nigga?"

Preach's men who walked in quietly when no one was watching, tried to stop the melee but Derrick got involved and shoved one back. "Let him talk! He not gonna hurt him!"

For the moment they backed off. Besides, with Banks dead, Mason was the boss.

"Where...is...the...body?" Mason asked again.

"He's gone, man!" Preach said in a heavy whisper. "I promise, he's gone. He, he, couldn't, he couldn't make it because there was too much fluid on his brain. I'm so sorry. I'm so fucking sorry."

"That's not what I asked!" Mason said louder. "Where is the body? Where is he? I want to see him for myself."

"He's gone."

"Don't make me ask again?" He pressed the weapon to his forehead so hard his skin dented. His hand trembled he was so mad. One wrong move and he'd be shot spot on.

"I buried him. Because you told me if something happened, you wouldn't be able to do it. Remember? I was doing it for you!"

The room grew darker.

He did remember.

"He's gone, man. I swear he is."

Mason rolled off of him and hit the floor. He wept loudly.

It was a pain he would take with him for the rest of his life.

CHAPTER FIFTEEN
THE PETIT ESTATE
1972

*G*ina walked into the attic where Angela remained for months. She was surprised when she opened the door that Angela stood in front of her, almost as if she was waiting. Angela's arms were behind her back and hands clasped together.

"How are you?" Gina asked. Her eyes roamed over the space her daughter lived which was surprisingly neat despite how grungy it had been in the past.

Angela smiled. "I'm okay, mother. Thank you for asking."

"Are you hungry?"

"What you provide is plenty. So, I'm fine, mother."

Gina took a deep breath. "You know it's because of you and your dirty ways that I had to put you up here for so long right?"

"Yes, I understand. Finally."

"Even if I were to believe that you found those panties or books in your father's private area you still violated our trust. You entered our room and that alone meant you deserved repercussions."

"I am aware, mother. My isolation is definitely my fault."

"You're right. And I was so betrayed by you."

"I'm sorry for disappointing you, mother."

"I just was so angry, Angie."

"I know and I couldn't see that at first but now it's all clear. It was so unfair of me to put you in an uncomfortable position. But I'm learning, mother. I swear I'm learning."

Gina took a deep breath. She was pleased that Angela seemed to be coming along the right way.

Her way.

"Okay I'm going to bring a television up here. So that you have something to give yourself a little mental vacation."

"That would be nice. And very considerate of you. Seeing as though you don't have to give me such luxuries."

Angela was saying all the right things. Which was a long way from her attitude months earlier. "Your father is not too pleased with you. After you exposed yourself at dinner. But he's willing to allow me to give you this one leniency."

"I am aware, mother. Please tell daddy I am sorry too."

Gina nodded and went downstairs.

The moment she was certain her mother was gone; she ran to the window where Peteery was outside in the neighbor's lawn. Intrigued as always, she raised the window and sat on the sill to get a better view.

If she fell, she would die instantly.

A wide smile spread across her face because for that moment she had peace.

With nothing but time, she thought about her life over the months of being in isolation. She felt smarter. Stronger. In that period, she learned a lot from the book on brainwashing. And as a result, she knew all the right answers to provide Gina in order to be free.

When Peteery saw her face, he waved. They had since learned a silent way of communicating if Gina was home. It wasn't similar to sign language. That was too advanced. But they understood each other all the same.

When he saw his lover's face, he removed his shirt and she removed hers.

He smiled and signed with his hands.

She shook her head no, because she was aware of what he wanted.

He smiled brighter and mouthed, "Please."

She giggled and then removed her bra. She liked to make him wait.

And the moment he saw her flesh he mouthed, "You're perfect."

She blushed.

When Gina got in her car, he could see her driving away, and so he pretended to be attending Mrs. Fischer's grounds.

Angie hid.

The moment she was gone he could talk loudly. "She's gone! And I can't wait any longer. I need to be with you. I need to have you in my arms. We have to be together. This is no longer working for me."

She understood but was hurt.

Besides, she was young.

What could she do?

In her mind the relationship they shared was bizarre. It was a love that bloomed from her window. They never touched. Barely spoke due to being afraid of being heard. And were left to hold onto visions in their mind of what being together would be like.

By T. Styles

But he wanted more.

It was obvious.

"What do you want me to do?" She mouthed.

"I need you to make that decision."

She nodded. "Okay. Soon we will be together."

"How soon?"

"Very soon."

CHAPTER SIXTEEN
THE PETIT ESTATE
THE NEXT DAY

Minnesota and Spacey sat at the dinner table with Gina and Hercules. It was a weird meal that left unanswered questions and a sense of awkwardness in the air.

Wiping her mouth with a tattered linen cloth Gina said, "Are you ready to see Banks? To see how she's doing?"

They nodded yes although they were tiring of hearing her improper use of pronouns.

"Very much." Minnesota said.

"Me too." Spacey answered.

To be honest he didn't like the feel of the place and wanted any reason to get away from the dining room table and house. While they were there, they tried several times to use their cell phones. To let others, know where they were. But they didn't work. It was as if they were cut off on purpose.

"Are you okay, Gina?" Minnesota asked. "You look bad."

"Feel like I have a fever, but I'll be fine." She scooted back in her chair. "Let's go."

By T. Styles

When Gina was leading them toward Banks' room Spacey pulled Minnesota to the side by tugging lightly on her elbow. "Is it me or do you feel like something's off?"

She looked to make sure Gina wasn't near and whispered, "I do. But dad is here, and I need to make sure he's okay tonight."

"Me too. I just wish we could call Preach and Mason. You know what I mean? To let them know where we are."

"But you agreed not to say a word, Spacey. If we do that, she may not help dad. You see how good he looks now."

"You're right. But something's off, Minnesota. And I don't want to stay another day."

"You think she's doing something with the phones?"

"I don't know. All I know is she went through a lot to get us here. And it makes me uncomfortable."

"Are you coming?" Gina asked startling them both. "To see your...mothe...Banks?"

"Oh, yes, we're coming now." Spacey said awkwardly while smiling.

A few seconds later they were in Banks' room as the doctor took his pressure. He looked so much better they couldn't help but feel slightly relieved.

It made the weirdness surrounding Gina a little worth the trouble.

But his eyes were still closed, and he hadn't regained consciousness.

The doctor dropped the stethoscope around his neck. "His vitals are good. But it doesn't mean he's in the clear."

"Well at least he doesn't look how he did yesterday." Spacey said. "I know it's not a lot, but we'll take it."

"Yeah, it was very scary." Minnesota said.

"I just want to make sure you both understand that being in the clear doesn't mean he will be back to his old self." The doctor was firm and realistic. "We won't know what Banks' new normal is until he wakes up."

"You can leave us alone now, doctor." Gina said.

He nodded and walked away.

"Well, we're already making progress." Gina said rubbing her hands together. "It's a good thing you called me, right?"

She was about to touch Banks until Minnesota said, "You look bad. Maybe you shouldn't touch him. We wouldn't want him catching anything you got."

By T. Styles

Gina nodded and coughed. "You're right."

Minnesota and Spacey nodded.

"Well, before you leave, did you want to see where your grandmother lived? You know how important it is for me that you know your family's history."

"Just because we know, doesn't mean we'll want a relationship with you." Spacey said as if she were his real grandmother too. But that was the way Banks raised them. "Because right now, trust is still broken."

"I get it. I just figured it would be nice."

Minnesota looked at Spacey. To be honest they hadn't really thought about Angela because they never knew her.

"Sure." He shrugged. "Why not?"

A minute later they were at the top of the house in the garret. "Wow, this place is massive." Minnesota said.

"Grandmother stayed here?" Spacey asked suspiciously?

"Yes. And despite what you feel, she liked this space very much. Maybe I'll let you read some of the letters she wrote while here."

"Why would she have to write you letters?" Minnesota frowned.

Gina smiled.

It was weird.

Minnesota walked over to the large window on the other side of the garret. Looking down at the lawn she sighed deeply. "It's a nice view."

"Your grandmother felt the same way."

Spacey wasn't feeling the spot. It made him sad. "Um, do you, like know when pops will be taken to a hospital? At least so they can look at him and make sure he's good? I like the doctor you got but..."

"Ready to leave already?" Gina asked, clasping her hands in front of her.

"Yeah." He nodded. "Kinda."

She took a deep breath. "Let me ask the doctor. I'll be right back."

Gina turned around and closed the door.

When she was gone Spacey said, "This place feels crazy. I want to get out of here."

"Try your cell phone again." Minnesota responded. "We higher up. It might work."

Spacy tried to make a phone call and so did Minnesota to no avail. "Fuck, it's still not working."

"Let me ask her straight up what's going on because I'm not feeling this shit." Spacey responded.

By T. Styles

When they walked over to the door, they were surprised it was locked. Spacey shook the knob left and right but it wouldn't budge.

"Turn it again!" Minnesota yelled standing behind him.

"That's what I'm trying to do. But it won't open."

"Well try harder!"

"You know what, why don't you try." He stepped out the way. "Since you obviously don't believe me."

Minnesota stepped up and tried to open the door. She was also unsuccessful. At that point they looked at one another.

Could this be the beginning of a whole new dark world?

JERSEY'S ESTATE

Mason, Preach and Joey stood in the lawn on Jersey's property where Preach claimed Banks' body was buried. It was as if they were having a funeral.

Life was getting grimmer. For instance, Preach had taken his father home due to his condition worsening. And now, even he was feeling ill himself. Feverish and weak. Due to the situation, he figured it was his nerves.

And then there was Joey who was so overcome with grief that he hadn't said a word since learning of his father's death. And what made matters worse was that he couldn't find his brother and sister to tell them the horrible news.

When Joey finally chose to speak, he said, "I, I can't do this. I, I really have to go. I need, I need to go."

Mason sighed. "Where you going, son?"

Joey frowned. "First off, I'm not a project!" He yelled. "You don't have to treat me like one."

Mason knew where the pain originated so he didn't take his outburst personally. In fact, he could barely manage himself due to being devastated. And at the same time, he needed Joey and the others to know that he had all intentions on remaining in their lives.

"I know you're not a project."

"We both know," Preach added.

By T. Styles

"I just need you to know I'm here." Mason continued.

Joey nodded and walked out.

Preach took a deep breath. "We going to feel this for a long time. A really long time."

Mason sighed. "I'm not alive. I'm dead. Just...gone..."

"I want to talk to you about something." Preach said.

"What is it?"

"I, I think you should let the twins stay with Gina."

Mason frowned. "Why the fuck would I do that?"

"Look at everything that happened? Look at everything that's been happening. We can't bring babies into another round of this shit. We street niggas. Do you want the boys to be too?"

"This is the family they were born into."

"I get that. But don't they deserve a chance? At a real life?"

"First off I don't even know who this crazy bitch *really* is. So why would I let my sons stay with her?"

"I, I just think you should think about it that's all."

Mason shook his head. "That's easy for you to say. They ain't your responsibilities."

"Please don't say that shit to me."

"Say what?"

"You acting like I don't care about them."

"Nigga, I'm feeling this pain on levels I haven't expressed to anyone. Ever! Like I really feel like I'm dreaming. Like I'm dead. Everything is a fog and I keep waiting to wake the fuck up! My best friend, the love of my life, my everything is gone. And now you want me to give up our sons too? I can't do that."

Preach took a deep breath. "You're right. I'm just thinking about Ace and Walid being so young. And impressionable. I wonder what may have happened if we had a chance at a real life. Maybe...maybe we would've been doctors or some shit like that. Maybe they can be doctors too."

"Nah, if I die, I'd come back as another street nigga. And so would my sons."

"Your decision is your own. Those are your boys. But they deserve a life away from this war shit. And, I guess, I just want you to think about it that's all."

By T. Styles

The night sky was spectacular as Bolero rode in the backseat of one of his cars being chauffeured. After trying to hit the Wales kids and missing, he had to rethink his whole operation and strategy. But first he had to find out where Mason and Banks rested their heads, which was easier said than done. He knew in his heart they were under his nose but in the moment, he was too angry and confused to think clearly.

All of a sudden, the car jumped.

Bolero frowned. "What was that?"

"I don't know." The driver looked out the rearview mirror.

"What do you mean you don't know?" He looked around from where he sat. "You're the one driving. Did you roll over something?"

The car bobbled along.

"Sir, it's so dark out here I really can't see straight." He squinted as if it would help his vision. "But it feels like the tires are flat."

The driver pulled over on the side of the road. The moment he did a cop car that he hadn't known was trailing him pulled up behind them.

"Oh no." The driver said. "We got trouble."

"Just remain calm. We're clean."

The driver nodded. "Okay, okay, sir."

The cop approached the back seat instead of the driver's side. Tapping the window with his flashlight he said, "Roll the window down."

The driver looked back at Bolero. "What should I do?"

"Roll it down so we can get out of here."

The driver quickly obeyed, lowering his window, causing a cool gush of air to roll inside.

"Put the back window down." The cop said to Bolero.

And without Bolero's authorization the driver complied with the officer and rolled Bolero's window down too. Exposing him fully. "Open the car door."

"What is this about?" Bolero asked as if he hadn't done many things to warrant being pulled over.

"Open the door and get out. I won't ask again." His hand hovered over his weapon.

When the door was unlocked Bolero was yanked out and within minutes thrown into the back of a police car.

When the driver exited to find out why, the cop removed his weapon and aimed. "Get back inside! Or I'll take you too!"

The driver quickly obeyed and the cop pulled off.

"Can you tell me what this is about?" Bolero asked.

"I'll tell you when you get to the place."

He frowned. "What is the place?"

"Don't worry about that now. It won't help you anyway."

Before Bolero knew it, he was on a dark road. His heart rate immediately sped up because he knew this was the end of his life. "Who's paying you? Is it Banks? Or Mason?"

Looking at him from the rearview mirror he calmly said, "No."

"Then who is it?" He asked, not believing for one minute he would get an answer.

"Gina Petit."

"Gina Petit?" He repeated, more confused than ever.

He'd never heard of the name and yet she appeared to be more powerful than anyone he had ever dealt with. Including himself, after all, she used a cop.

"Let me assure you that I can double...no triple whatever you're being given. So there really is no need to do this."

"I know."

The cop opened the bullet proof glass, shot him in the head before pulling his body out and stuffing him in an already pitted ditch.

CHAPTER SEVENTEEN
THE LOUISVILLE ESTATE
TWO WEEKS LATER

B anks' new baby girl was perfect. Jersey having given birth to his third child, experienced a love she didn't know was possible. If only there wasn't a dark cloud over the moment. Because a new, unseen element had made itself known to the world, taking Rev's life with it.

Since she didn't want to be alone, for the moment she was back at the Louisville Estate so that she could get some assistance. Sitting in the living room, Derrick and Mason showed their support for the little girl. While Shay sat on the recliner, looking out the window.

She was miserable.

She had so many questions. She wondered where was Minnesota? She wondered where was Spacey and why was his wife calling her every five minutes to find out?

She wondered about the Twins too.

She was angry and livid about it all.

She even reached out to Natty who appeared to have fallen off the face of the Earth. It was strange.

Every person she tried to contact made themselves ghosts and she didn't understand why.

"You talk to Preach?" Jersey asked.

Mason nodded.

"How's he doing?"

He shrugged. "As well as to be expected with his father dying." He paused. "We have to be careful out here. To make sure we don't get whatever this shit is going around."

Derrick sat by his mother on the couch, with a weird smile on his face that angered Shay greatly. After all, she thought he didn't like babies.

"I can't wait until she's old enough." Derrick said with a wide toothed grin. "So, I can show her how much I care about her."

"Give me a break," Shay said under her breath.

Jersey smiled at Derrick. "That's new. I thought babies weren't your thing."

"I know what you're thinking." He took a deep breath. "I wasn't this way with Ace and Walid. But this is my little sister. You know what I mean?" His eyes lit up. "We never had that in our family, and I want to make sure she's good."

"She isn't your blood," Shay said.

"Why should that matter?" He responded.

"Oh, so now blood is not a big deal? As much as you throw up in my face that I wasn't related to Banks? Nigga, you berserk."

"Stop it, Shay," Mason said.

"No, I won't! What is going on with everybody?"

"You need to calm down is what the fuck is going on." Derrick said.

"I won't! Are we going to pretend like Banks is really dead? Are we going to pretend that Ace and Walid are gone forever? And Minnesota? And Spacey? Because this ain't adding up."

Derrick was so angry he wanted to slap the dust off her face. "The baby only two weeks old and she don't need to hear all that yelling right now."

"I get all that." She wiped her nose with the back of her hand. "But I miss my family!"

"You tripping." Derrick said.

"Tripping? My father is gone! And I'm by myself!" She yelled standing up. "And I'm not gonna sit by and let ya'll dust off his memory."

"Ain't nobody doing all that!" Derrick yelled.

"That's how it feels to me!"

"Honey, he's gone." Jersey said as tears rolled down her cheeks. "And I know it's hard for you to understand. But we all saw Banks. His condition was grave and Preach is a good friend. Someone we trust with our lives. And if he says Banks is dead, we have to move on that. It's okay to be hurt but we are with you."

Shay plopped back down. "I, I don't believe him. I just don't." With a lowered gaze she said, "We should snatch Preach up and ask him a bit harder. I can do it myself."

Mason took the baby from Jersey's arm and sat on the other end of the sofa. In the moment, he was using the infant as a way to heal a very deep and penetrating pain. It also helped that she named the baby Blakeslee, after him. She resembled him already.

"I miss him so much," Shay said under her breath. "I miss Minnesota and Spacey too. And then the twins...where is every fucking body?" She looked at Jersey. "You claimed you were really their mother, but you don't even care."

"Banks is the mother remember?" Derrick said.

"Sometimes I can't believe I deal with you."

"Shay, the moment I know where Ace and Walid are, I *will* bring them home." Mason said. "Trust me. We just, we just moving in a different way right now until I can find out more information."

"Why it feels slow though?"

"Because I gotta, I gotta sort a lot of things out."

By T. Styles

"But, but what about Banks? Are you gonna find him too?"

"Banks is gone." Mason finally said. It was the first time he allowed himself to utter those words.

"I'm telling you he's alive. And I don't know why I feel that way. And I don't know why Minnesota and Spacey are gone. But something is off. I saw Joey the other day and he didn't say it, but I believe he's on drugs again. I hope I'm wrong. Either way, this is not what Banks would have wanted. We need to find him, and we need to get back together."

As Mason rocked the baby, he thought a lot about what she said. He was overwhelmed with grief. But it wasn't a complete pain. He assumed the partial feeling was because he hadn't seen his body. And so, feeling grateful for the small decency that Preach provided, mentally, to him, Banks was still alive.

But was she right?

Was he somewhere out there in need of help?

Derrick saw the look in his father's eye. "Aye, Pops, he dead. I see you over there thinking. Let it go."

"You sound crazy." Shay said. "If your bitch ass was gone, I bet you would want somebody to come looking for your crusty ass."

"But I ain't gone, am I?"

"I wish you were though," Shay said under her breath.

"Don't say that." Jersey said.

Derrick stood up and walked over to his father. "Pops, like I said, don't let this mess you up. We here. We need you. Even if Banks is alive, he may not want this life anymore. Minnesota and Spacey are gone. I'm sure Bolero killed them. And I know you gonna send the dogs out for the twins, but let Banks go."

"I really can't stand you." Shay said softly.

He looked back at her and focused on Mason. "Let it go, Pops. I'm begging."

Mason was silent.

But Shay was determined to be the final voice in his ear. "Mason, sir, he's alive. I feel it in my heart. Don't you feel it too?"

CHAPTER EIGHTEEN
THE PETIT ESTATE
1972

*W*ith time and isolation, Angela had become a very patient girl. No longer was she pushy and annoying to her mother. She realized that in order to get her freedom she had to play smart.

Besides she had read the book BRAINWASH LOVE by Gemma Holmes from front to back many times. And one of the steps discussed was how to know if you can trust the person being brainwashed.

There was an exercise that went over the victim's anxiousness. If the person being brainwashed was too excited to leave, or to get from up under the brainwasher's control, then at that time it was important to keep them isolated longer.

And so, every time Gina asked if she was ready to leave, she would say, "No. I only want to leave when you are willing or ready to allow me out."

Angela was so good that one-night Gina persisted that she at least come down for a meal. Instead of being overly excited she said, "Only if you want me to. I don't want to do anything against your will."

Because of her ability to remain calm, Gina was starting to let her guards down. She even left the door open a few times knowing that if she was faking, she would take the bait. But Angela remained in the garret refusing to leave. Knowing that in the end, she would be able to run away with Peteery and finally that day came.

One rainy night, Gina walked up the stairs and said, "How are you?"

"I'm fine, mother. Thank you."

Gina sighed. "We're going to service and I want you to come with us."

Angela said, "Only if you want me to. I don't want to do anything against you or your will."

Loving the answer, and the fact that Angela appeared to be bending, Gina smiled and said "It is my will. Today you sleep in your own room."

And so, later on that night, she slept in her own bed.

But when everyone was asleep, in the middle of the night she got up and returned to the garret. Taking some time, she etched some writing in the wood paneling surrounding the window. It could only be viewed if you looked closely.

By T. Styles

She didn't know why, but she was compelled to leave a message.

At first glance you would not be able to see the words. But they were definitely there. It said:

The secret to your freedom is not outside the window.
Love Angela

And with that she ran away.

Minnesota and Spacey were living in the garret above their great-grandmother's house. Gina didn't interact much with them, but what she did do was feed them a lot.

But unlike the fruits and vegetables that she gave Angela which eventually made her strong enough to escape, she fed them sugary snacks that were too hard to resist.

Life had been difficult, especially for Spacey.

In the beginning Minnesota tried to rebel, and each time she did, Spacey would be taken out of the garret, sometimes for days and beaten severely. As a result, he had a broken arm that was healing badly, and cigarette burns over thirty percent of his body.

Minnesota quickly learned that it was she that Gina was trying to get through to. And instead of hurting her, she would hurt her brother, which brought her great distress.

Since it was lunch time, when the maid came upstairs wearing a face mask to bring food, Spacey tried to escape. He was almost free, until Hercules ran up and shoved him back inside.

The moment the door closed; Minnesota who was now heavier by ten pounds rushed up to him. "What's wrong with you?"

Spacey frowned and looked at her as if she were crazy. "Wait, are you serious? We been locked up for months, Minnesota. And they been hurting me like I'm a—"

"I know! And that's why I want you to stop. It's not you that she wants but she'll use you to get to me."

"I can't be here, Minnesota."

"I get that. But there are better ways to handle shit." She took a deep breath and looked down. "At least, at least I hope so."

By T. Styles

He frowned. "Hold up, are you cool with us being up here forever?"

"Of course not, Spacey."

"Good, because I'm losing my mind. I don't...I don't like how I feel. I don't like the things I think about in the middle of the night. I don't like the emotions that stay with me always."

"What does that mean?"

"We have to get out of here. That's all I know. Okay?" He looked away feeling too guilty to tell her straight up about his terrible thoughts.

She walked up to him. "I don't know why but I feel it won't be long." She paused. "I feel like, like something or someone is guiding us. Which is why we got to be smart. We have to say less. I don't know great-grandmother's motives. Since she won't be clear but, but something will give soon."

"Why do you call her that?"

"Great-grandmother?"

"Yes."

She shrugged. "Because I have to convince myself that she doesn't mean us harm. Because if I think she's just some weird woman wanting to take away our freedom, I'll lose it too. And you don't want that."

"We don't even know what's going on with Pops."

"I believe he's okay. I just, I just do."

"So, you think he's up somewhere in this house? Without knowing we're upstairs?"

"I don't know. But I pray about it every night. I pray that if he is up, that he remembers us. That he comes looking for us."

"I'm fucked up in here, Minnesota. I really am."

"Me too. Yesterday I thought about so much. I thought about the things I did. The things I didn't respect. And I know everyone thinks I'm a brat. And to be honest I probably was. But this place, whatever it is, is changing me. I don't want to die."

"Well I wish you'd lose some weight too."

"Why are you so fascinated with my size all of a sudden?" She frowned.

He looked away.

"Listen, maybe we fucked up somewhere along the line, Spacey. But all we have right now is each other. Please try to make it easier on me. On *us*. At least until we figure this out."

He shook his head. "If you say so."

She smiled and squeezed his hand.

He quickly pulled away. "I have to go to the bathroom."

By T. Styles

When he walked off, she strolled up to the window and looked outside. She imagined what her grandmother must have felt like when she lived in the Attic.

She wondered why she was locked up against her will.

While looking out the window, suddenly she happened to see some writing. *The secret to your freedom is not outside the window. Love Angela.* She read to herself.

What does that mean? She thought.

When she squinted a little, she happened to see the edges of a wood paneling that appeared to be raised. After some tugging, she popped it open and her eyes widened when she saw something hidden inside.

Removing it quickly she saw it was a book, a magazine and a sock snake. Her eyes widened. Finally, she was given hope. Tucking the book behind her back she smiled.

Just then Spacey exited the bathroom. "What you happy about?"

"I believe Grandmother just gave us the answer to our prayers."

Mason was on the balcony outside overlooking the mountainous terrain in Deep Creek Maryland. Inside the house were a bunch of strangers he didn't know disguised as Dasher's friends. Truth be told he didn't want to be in such large gatherings, as social distancing was the new norm, but he was doing it for his girl.

And then there was what he considered a much more important issue.

Mason was attempting to bring himself back to life after losing Banks. He even tried to feel something inside again by moving forward with his new relationship. But it was hard.

Banks was always on his mind.

He was also angry because at the moment he was drinking wine and was tiring of the taste. What he really wanted was one glass of whiskey for old time sake, like he used to share with Banks. But she didn't plan in advance and so he didn't have any available.

By T. Styles

Looking up at the stars that were twinkling bright he said, "Banks, if you alive I need a sign."

Silence.

"A sign specifically for me. A sign that only I will know or understand, and I need it right now."

He spoke from his heart because what he didn't tell a soul, was that after talking to Shay, he went as far as to dig up the earth behind Jersey's estate just to get proof that Banks' corpse was beneath. But when he dug at the mounds nothing was there. Later, Preach told him he had the bodies removed for fear that someone would come searching and he wanted to believe him.

But he couldn't.

And so, still ripped up, he desired some sign that his friend was out there. Because if he had one, just one, he would risk hell and earth to find him.

"Talk to me, Banks."

Just then Dasher opened the balcony door and came outside.

He looked back at her and then at the mountains. "Having a good time?" He asked.

"I was at first."

"What changed?"

"I'm worried about you." Taking a deep breath, she said, "Oh yeah, guess what I found just now."

Mason wasn't in the mood, but he played along. "What?"

"Whiskey. It was in the back of the bar. The thing is, I could have sworn we looked there before but I didn't see it. Want a glass?"

Mason smiled having gotten his answer.

And what he didn't realize was that in one state over, at that exact moment, Banks Wales opened his eyes.

Hooked up to an oxygen tank for what would surely be the rest of her life, Gina had a rough couple of months. Having contracted an unknown virus, at first, she was down for the count and it looked as if she may die. But with rest, water and treatment, she was back on the scene although her life would never be the same.

I guess it was true that evil never dies.

Now, sitting in the boardroom of Strands Inc, she was trying to prevent them from voting her out of the company she helped create. She needed these drastic measures to stop. After all, she was broker than normal, a fact she kept away from everyone even her sons. Her company was the only thing she held near.

At the same time, her idea of broke meant she only had a million to spare.

Her decrease in wealth didn't stop the stockholder's concerns. Shares had dropped because the world had changed. No one was interested in using serums or hiding their bald heads under wigs, electing to showcase them instead, as a way to say I fought cancer and won.

But Gina was brilliant.

Throughout the years she had been watching the trends. And there was one that continued to grow despite it all. African American natural hair care. Years ago, when she saw this scene booming, she wanted to delve into the market.

But, how could she?

She needed two things.

First, she needed knowledge of this growing community. She was the best in the business to that end and as a result, dived into the market and created a product she was sure would stun.

Secondly, she needed a face for her brand.

Not just any face. A face that would lead its lineage right back to the Petit family. Which was a trusted product. And now, she had that too.

After the stockholders reviewed the proposal Gina prepared, she smiled. "Gentlemen, allow me to introduce Strong Curls Inc. Using the steps and investment strategies outlined herein, we will rule the world."

"I notice this plan is contingent upon building this brand around Petit family members," one stockholder said.

Through the breathing mask she said proudly, "That is true. Petit is a trusted brand and it will remain so."

He looked at the rest of the members. "But correct me if I'm wrong, last I checked you were well...white."

They all laughed.

She smiled and raised her head higher. "My family extends far and wide. You will find out, soon."

By T. Styles

When Banks opened his eyes, shocked, the doctor who was checking his pressure ran out of the room and grabbed Gina.

During the months that passed, many things happened in his body biologically. His curly hair had grown considerably and stretched past the bottom of his ear. His beard was gone, and his face was smooth due to keeping it shaved regularly. Besides, since he was no longer on hormone therapy, his facial hair was less coarse and required fewer shavings.

In a matter of speaking, his masculine features were weakening causing his natural beauty to shine through.

Rushing to his bedside, dragging her tank, Gina said, "How are you?" She touched his hand.

Banks opened and closed his mouth as he tried to form a sentence. Just as Hercules and Aaron entered.

"Are you okay?" Gina asked Banks again, praying his memory would fail him.

Banks looked around from where he lay and took a deep breath. In a soft whisper he asked, "Who...who am I?"

EPILOGUE
ONE YEAR LATER
WINTER

The snow was falling as Mason sat in a large refrigerated water truck cruising down Palm Lane in Richmond Virginia. His cell phone sat in his lap on speaker to communicate with the caller. To disguise himself, his upper lip was covered with a thick fake mustache and he was wearing a blue Artic White uniform and hat.

At first glance he would definitely be unrecognizable.

"I don't see the house you described, man." He said, as he zeroed in on each multi-million-dollar home he passed. "This shit ain't adding up."

"I'm telling you, they said it was off that lane." Johnathan said. "I wouldn't make this shit up."

"And are they...are they..." He couldn't complete the sentence because having hope was too much to bare. After all, since getting the info about the sighting, he had been trying for weeks to locate the home. "Are they sure they saw my sons?"

"Mason, on everything they said it was them."

"Give me verbatim again."

By T. Styles

He sighed. "Okay, so they said they think they saw Ace and Walid with this older white man. So, they followed him to that area and the cops ran my niggas away before they could follow him to the house. I guess rich folks complained about two niggas being on the block and made the call. So, I got the information they gave me and called you."

"If them niggas lying I'ma fuck you and them up." He hung up.

He had a reason to be angry.

Lately it appeared that everyone with a bill knew he was searching for his sons and they used his desire to know where they were to make a come up. After all, he was paying big money for answers. Over the year most leads ended in vain but this time, he felt the info came from a credible source.

On his word, Mason drove up and down the block which only included three homes. All properties were surrounded by huge black iron wrought gates. Like the hood niggas before him, he was also drawing unwanted attention and was about to leave when suddenly two little boys bolted out of large doubled doors connected to a massive stone ridge house.

He was so stunned that he almost ran into a mail truck in front of him.

Slowly he parked at the curb.

It was easy to see why he almost crashed. Because at that moment he was looking at his flesh and blood, his beautiful little sons. Their thick curly hair blasted through the LV knit caps they wore and bounced as they moved.

While gazing at them with love, his breath felt trapped in his throat, but he couldn't help but smile. Their light skin was bright and healthy, and they were dressed in leather coats and designer clothing. If youngsters could look like money, they fit the bill. Their personalities were also coming into view. Although Ace wore a look of joy and happiness, Walid seemed laid back as if observing his surroundings.

In fact, he was the one who spotted Mason in the truck. To be so young, he appeared wise beyond his years. As if drawn to him, slowly he walked through the white hilly snow, in the direction of the vehicle.

"Oh shit," Mason said ducking down. "Does he, does he recognize me?"

"Walid, no!" A woman called out.

When Mason heard the voice, he was shocked and stunned. Because the sound was familiar, although somewhat changed.

By T. Styles

What he saw next brought everything into complete understanding.

Slowly he rose and his heart thumped when he realized he was looking at Banks Wales. Except so much had changed.

He, or *she*, was drop dead gorgeous.

His curly thick hair appeared healthy and hung at his shoulders. Despite the chocolate fur coat he wore, Mason could still see what appeared to be a curvaceous shape coming into view with the fit long dress he was wearing.

He felt faint.

This was how he pictured him in his mind.

Was this even real?

He was so sick; he pushed the driver's door opened and vomited on the ground. With heavy breath, when he finished, he closed the door softly, only to see Banks approaching the truck.

While Walid, a child of very few faces...smiled.

Before Banks could reach the vehicle, Mason threw the car in drive and pulled away from the scene.

To say he was enraged was an understatement.

Because Banks being alive meant Preach lied. It also meant Gina was a snake for how she'd done his friend. And it meant life as he knew it would change, once again.

By T. Styles

CARTEL PUBLICATIONS

PRESENTS

The Cartel Publications Order Form
www.thecartelpublications.com
Inmates **ONLY** receive novels for $10.00 per book **PLUS** shipping fee **PER BOOK.**
(Mail Order **MUST** come from inmate directly to receive discount)

Shyt List 1	_____	$15.00
Shyt List 2	_____	$15.00
Shyt List 3	_____	$15.00
Shyt List 4	_____	$15.00
Shyt List 5	_____	$15.00
Shyt List 6	_____	$15.00
Pitbulls In A Skirt	_____	$15.00
Pitbulls In A Skirt 2	_____	$15.00
Pitbulls In A Skirt 3	_____	$15.00
Pitbulls In A Skirt 4	_____	$15.00
Pitbulls In A Skirt 5	_____	$15.00
Victoria's Secret	_____	$15.00
Poison 1	_____	$15.00
Poison 2	_____	$15.00
Hell Razor Honeys	_____	$15.00
Hell Razor Honeys 2	_____	$15.00
A Hustler's Son	_____	$15.00
A Hustler's Son 2	_____	$15.00
Black and Ugly	_____	$15.00
Black and Ugly As Ever	_____	$15.00
Ms Wayne & The Queens of DC **(LGBT)**	_____	$15.00
Black And The Ugliest	_____	$15.00
Year Of The Crackmom	_____	$15.00
Deadheads	_____	$15.00
The Face That Launched A Thousand Bullets	_____	$15.00
The Unusual Suspects	_____	$15.00
Paid In Blood	_____	$15.00
Raunchy	_____	$15.00
Raunchy 2	_____	$15.00
Raunchy 3	_____	$15.00
Mad Maxxx (4th Book Raunchy Series)	_____	$15.00
Quita's Dayscare Center	_____	$15.00
Quita's Dayscare Center 2	_____	$15.00
Pretty Kings	_____	$15.00
Pretty Kings 2	_____	$15.00
Pretty Kings 3	_____	$15.00
Pretty Kings 4	_____	$15.00
Silence Of The Nine	_____	$15.00
Silence Of The Nine 2	_____	$15.00
Silence Of The Nine 3	_____	$15.00

WAR 7: PINK COTTON   265

Prison Throne	_____	$15.00
Drunk & Hot Girls	_____	$15.00
Hersband Material **(LGBT)**	_____	$15.00
The End: How To Write A	_____	$15.00
Bestselling Novel In 30 Days (Non-Fiction Guide)		
Upscale Kittens	_____	$15.00
Wake & Bake Boys	_____	$15.00
Young & Dumb	_____	$15.00
Young & Dumb 2: Vyce's Getback	_____	$15.00
Tranny 911 **(LGBT)**	_____	$15.00
Tranny 911: Dixie's Rise **(LGBT)**	_____	$15.00
First Comes Love, Then Comes Murder	_____	$15.00
Luxury Tax	_____	$15.00
The Lying King	_____	$15.00
Crazy Kind Of Love	_____	$15.00
Goon	_____	$15.00
And They Call Me God	_____	$15.00
The Ungrateful Bastards	_____	$15.00
Lipstick Dom **(LGBT)**	_____	$15.00
A School of Dolls **(LGBT)**	_____	$15.00
Hoetic Justice	_____	$15.00
KALI: Raunchy Relived	_____	$15.00
(5th Book in Raunchy Series)		
Skeezers	_____	$15.00
Skeezers 2	_____	$15.00
You Kissed Me, Now I Own You	_____	$15.00
Nefarious	_____	$15.00
Redbone 3: The Rise of The Fold	_____	$15.00
The Fold (4th Redbone Book)	_____	$15.00
Clown Niggas	_____	$15.00
The One You Shouldn't Trust	_____	$15.00
The WHORE The Wind		
Blew My Way	_____	$15.00
She Brings The Worst Kind	_____	$15.00
The House That Crack Built	_____	$15.00
The House That Crack Built 2	_____	$15.00
The House That Crack Built 3	_____	$15.00
The House That Crack Built 4	_____	$15.00
Level Up **(LGBT)**	_____	$15.00
Villains: It's Savage Season	_____	$15.00
Gay For My Bae	_____	$15.00
War	_____	$15.00
War 2: All Hell Breaks Loose	_____	$15.00
War 3: The Land Of The Lou's	_____	$15.00
War 4: Skull Island	_____	$15.00
War 5: Karma	_____	$15.00
War 6: Envy	_____	$15.00
War 7: Pink Cotton	_____	$15.00

(**Redbone 1** & **2** are **NOT** Cartel Publications novels and if **ordered** the cost is **FULL** price of $15.00 **each**. **No Exceptions**.)

Please add **$5.00** for shipping and handling fees for up to **(2) BOOKS PER ORDER**. (INMATES INCLUDED)

By T. Styles

(See Next Page for ORDER DETAILS)

The Cartel Publications * P.O. BOX 486 OWINGS MILLS MD 21117

Name: _____

Address: _____

City/State: _____

Contact/Email: _____

Please allow 8-10 BUSINESS days Before shipping.

The Cartel Publications is NOT responsible for Prison Orders rejected!

NO RETURNS and NO REFUNDS
NO PERSONAL CHECKS ACCEPTED
STAMPS NO LONGER ACCEPTED